Krystina Coles

Moonshadow

Copyright © 2019 by Krystina Coles

Front Cover Image by Kodey Bell, a.k.a Imaginesto

To My Father

Thank you for igniting my love for mythology with your own. I would not have this passion for writing without you. Also, thank you for coming into my room as Ghostface when I was five. I wouldn't be this mentally disturbed without you.

To Melissa

The fire to my ice

(You know what I mean)

To My Mother

Your horrified expressions after reading my writing let me know that I was headed in the right direction. Thank you for your sacrifices as a military mom and not being overly perturbed with my fascination for the macabre.

And

To Yasmen

I see you in the stars

CONTENTS

Prologue

There is a world beside our own, hidden in the twilight—the inbetween. Born within the boundaries of what is and what could be, buried deep inside hearts that yearn for more than what is merely seen. It lives in our impossible thoughts, fantastical dreams, mortal fears. We think we can contain it, but it is just as wild as the things that it produces: gods, goddesses, giants, fairies, demons. Our imagination—is there anything more powerful?

Chapter One

Eleven Ghosts

Cedar Crest, Oklahoma 2009

Every night, I drown; and every morning, I'm pulled from the water — only to die again when I reach the surface. They say that it's peaceful — like falling asleep; but the anguish in the struggle for the life that I knew could no longer be mine terrified me beyond my nightmares and found its way into my reality. I scream; but in the darkness, I can still see the world around me. And there is nothing but the silence of my isolation. I open my mouth to cry out again, reaching towards the salvation I couldn't hope to touch; and I'm pulled back into the blackness of the unknown — where I stay. And where my ghosts come to find me.

There was a knock at the door; and I sat up,

pushing my dark brown hair away from my eyes. I had fallen asleep again. But even as I came to my senses, I could still feel the water clawing at my neck—filling my lungs as I flailed my arms toward the rippling light of the surface.

"Melissa…Melissa, honey, it's time to go to school." I could hear her voice on the other side. My mother. She meant well. I knew she did. "Honey, are you awake?" I tiredly rubbed my forehead with the palm of my hand. I had almost forgotten what day it was. Wednesday— it was a Wednesday.

"Just a little longer." I shouted to her. *Just a couple more minutes.* I just needed a couple more minutes.

"All right." She called back to me through the door. "But Connor's already waiting for you downstairs." Connor. I glanced at the picture frame on my bedside table—at the three of us. I shut my eyes to smother the tears before they began and took a deep breath before pulling the drawer open and setting it inside. I didn't know why I hadn't done it sooner, but I guessed I didn't want to admit it just yet.

Eleven months—it'd been eleven months. But I still remembered screaming. And crying. And then doing nothing at all.

I had woken up that Monday morning

and gotten ready for school: taken a shower, brushed my teeth, picked out my clothes. It was a regular day. But in these past few months, I've realized news like that always comes when you least expect it — when the day begins like any other. I just didn't know it yet.

I had hurried down the stairs with my backpack in hand, knowing I'd have to skip breakfast to make it to school on time. Connor would be waiting for me in the living room — probably talking to my father about going out onto the lake and fishing in the spring; and Heather would be sharing Mrs. Harrison's famous croissants with my mother. But when I had reached the bottom of the stairs, the living room was quiet; and the kitchen was empty. I had called out to my mother, and she had answered; but the moment she'd spoken, I'd known something was wrong. She and my father had been sitting on the couch, and they had asked me to join them. I didn't want to, I'd told them. I'd just wanted to know where Heather and Connor were. But Connor was home, and Heather wasn't coming.

"There you are." My father looked up from his armchair, and Connor left his seat on the couch to head towards the door.

"C'mon. We're gonna be late." He told me, and I slung my backpack over my shoulder before moving to follow him.

"Melissa." I stopped and turned when my mother called my name. "Have a good day at school." I nodded, not really saying anything. What could I say? Nowadays, a little smile made her happy; and I found myself trying harder—if only for her. I closed the door behind me and locked it, standing there for a moment—wishing I didn't have to leave.

"Hey." Connor punched my arm to get my attention. "You okay?"

"Yeah." I waived it off, smiling.

"Good morning, Melissa!" I turned my head to the right to see my neighbor retrieving his newspaper from his doorstep. Dressed only in his robe and pajamas, I wondered how the old man could stand the cold.

"Good morning, Mr. Oakman!" I shouted back to him on the other side of the hedge of rosebushes that separated our front yards. He grinned at my response and waved goodbye before retreating back into his little blue house. "Are you ready for tonight?" I asked Connor when we reached the green Oldsmobile parked on the side of the curb. He paused for a second and then gave me one of his goofy grins.

"Yeah, I'm ready." I eyed him

suspiciously.

"You hesitated." He shrugged his shoulders like he didn't know what I was talking about.

"No, I didn't."

"Liar." Who did he think he was fooling? It definitely wasn't me. I pulled the door open and slid into the passenger seat. "Don't freak out. It's no big deal."

"I'm not." He insisted. I glanced at him again. "Really." He closed the car door and pulled his seatbelt over his chest. The car sputtered to life when he turned the key in the ignition, and I rolled down the window to watch my house disappear from view. The car turned the corner, passing a yellow house on the left; and I stared out into the empty driveway. Voices echoed in my mind; and for a moment, I saw two little princesses running away from a boy in a pirate costume.

"How do you think they're doing?"

"What?" His voice pulled me out of the well of memories I'd found myself in, and he ran his fingers through his short blond hair as he asked me again.

"How long has it been since you talked to

them?" I bit my lip at his words and swallowed.

"A while..." It hurt to say. My eyes started to burn with tears, but I blinked them away. "Maybe a couple months." But I remembered. It'd been four months. I'd come by on her birthday and spent an hour in her room...just to close my eyes and hear her voice again.

"Maybe we should drop by." Connor shrugged his shoulders again as he drove, staring at the road ahead.

"Have you seen Matthew since—" I wasn't sure if I could finish. I had seen him that cold January morning, still holding on to the stem of a little yellow flower when everyone else had gone.

"We cross paths at school, sometimes; but we don't say much." He answered.

The streets of Cedar Crest had faded away into the highway that passed the little town by. There was nothing but trees—and the vast expanse of a world untouched around us. Just dirt and sky. We passed a few houses every once in a while...the kind I wouldn't enjoy approaching in the middle of the night. Old and dilapidated, they stood like tombstones scattered over the barren countryside; and I tried to imagine the kind of people that lived in them.

Were they ancient and crotchety? Did they argue over simple things—like whose turn it was to hold the baby when he cried? Did they have a daughter who loved to play hide-and-seek in the woods?

Did she die too?

I leaned my head against the car door and breathed in the cold crisp air that came rushing in through the window.

"Maybe we should." They all wanted me to get over it—forget. But Connor understood. He was the only one who could. I glanced at him from my seat and wondered. If he ever cried, I didn't see it. He caught me staring and flashed a reassuring grin, punching my arm again as he laughed.

"You gotta smile." He insisted. "'Cause if you don't, I *will* self-destruct." That would be a sight.

"So you *are* nervous." I crossed my arms, satisfied with the momentary flicker of emotion he had shown me.

"I didn't say that." He denied it, but the devious glance he gave me said otherwise. As we crossed the last stretch of water before entering Locust Grove, I gazed at the hands of the Neosho River reaching out into the earth beneath me. And in the surface, I saw my reflection—as fleeting as it was—rippling in the water below. And once again, I was grasping at nothing, slowly sinking into darkness.

The slamming of the car door startled me from my nightmare, and I was sitting in the parking lot of the high school. I squinted my eyes in the sudden burst of sunlight when Connor opened the door.

"Are you ready to go?" I paused before I answered, gathering my senses.

"Yeah." I unfastened my seatbelt and stepped down from the car onto solid ground, and we hurried to join the wave of red and white as it funneled into the halls. There were nearly five hundred of us in all. Not in the sophomore class—no—but in the school in its entirety. Locust Grove was small, but it still somehow managed to be three times the size of Cedar Crest. I couldn't imagine what a high school dance in our town would look like. Connor and I parted ways, promising to make it to World History early so we could find seats next to each other. It wouldn't be hard. There were only sixteen in the class. I followed my classmates through the third door on the left and sat down at one of the desks in the back of the room, hoping I'd be less conspicuous there. I didn't mind it when Mr. Thompson called on me, but I could tell the others did. Their bewildered stares and looks of alarm on their faces said it all. They thought I was slipping, withering away. Maybe I was.

"Good morning—" Mr. Thompson began, but he was interrupted by the high-pitched screech of the school bell; and we stood to recite the words we learned when we were too young to spell our names.

"Have an Argh-mazing day!" It was the last we heard of the voice on the intercom, and I smiled to myself. The cheerleaders always made the announcements on game day. If there was anything that I missed, it was starting the day with ridiculous puns and eating donuts in the principal's office.

"Good morning, class." Mr. Thompson started again as he gripped a stick of chalk to write on the forest green board behind him. "We are going to begin with a review of what we accomplished last month," he took a step forward when he was finished, revealing a word that wouldn't have made sense to anyone else if we hadn't taken his class. "NaNoWriMo." He said, leaning on his desk and holding a stack of papers over his head. "Now, most of you did a pretty good job; and you know I won't give out anything less than an 'A' if you tried your best, but there are a few of you who could use a little more inspiration." He strolled through the rows of chairs, laying the graded papers on my classmates' desks. "I'm not going to name names, but…" He stopped to look at the boy sitting in front of me. "Jason." He gave him the caricature of a stern glance, and the room erupted in a hush of giggles. From over his shoulder, I could see the letter 'D' in bright red, and I sucked in the air through my teeth. "Miss Moonwater…" Mr. Thompson called my name to claim my attention. "Congratulations." He grinned as he handed me the packet of stapled paper, adding, "as always." I breathed a sigh of relief at the 'A' written neatly in the upper right corner. "Now that you've gotten back your papers, how do think you could improve your novels-in-the-making?" He returned to the front of the class and waited for a response. There was none. "Anyone?" Silence. I raised my hand, immediately regretting it. "Yes, Miss Moonwater?" He crossed his arms in anticipation.

"Well," I ignored the heads that turned to set their eyes on me, "you told us to write what we know." It sounded like a question more than an answer. He clapped his hands together so suddenly, I jumped in my seat.

"That's right." He hurried to the chalkboard to write down my words and turned expectantly. "So what do you know?" Another boy in a red and white Letterman jacket raised his hand in the second row.

"Yes, Mister Hughes?"

Kris. Inches taller than anyone else in the class, he was the only senior in my elective. With dark brown hair that hung over his sky blue eyes, nearly every girl in the sophomore class had become infatuated with him. Lately, I'd seen him in the hallway with Adrienne Shelley, the self-proclaimed future prom queen of a dance two years away—but that didn't stop her from campaigning.

"What about the Twelve Dancing Princesses?" It seemed like an odd question. A strange quietness descended over the class like a blanket, and he fell silent when he realized that he had made a mistake. It wasn't something we talked about. What used to be the title of an innocent fairytale had become the town's affliction, as if Mayes County had taken up the mantle of that faraway kingdom only to realize its twisted truth much too late to return it.

"Okay." Mr. Thompson broke the silence, suddenly somber. "We all know the original story, don't we?" It was quiet, and he scratched his head. "All right. The story was published by the Brothers Grimm in 1812." He began, and I swallowed in apprehension as he continued. "In the tale, a king used to lock the door to the room where his twelve daughters slept; and every morning, he would discover that their shoes were worn to pieces. The king, concerned by this, promised his kingdom to anyone who could uncover his daughters' secret; but those who failed would be put to death."

"That sucks." Jaxon Haymes said from the corner of the room.

"It does." Mr. Thompson pointed his stick of chalk at him as he agreed and went on. "But one man, a soldier returning from war, was able to uncover their secret. In the middle of the night, the princesses would leave their room through a trap door in the floor; and they would travel through the forest to a lake where twelve princes would take them to a secret ball on the other side."

"So what—Rebecca Lawrence and Iliana Lopez are just out partying somewhere?" Kris quipped, skeptical. I held my breath at the sound of their names. Three months ago, they were sitting in this classroom.

"No, I'm afraid their disappearances are a little more on the darker side." He wove his way through the rows of desks as he spoke. "So what do we know about them?"

"The newscasters said that there have

been ten so far." Another student said, and he nodded.

"That's right." He retreated to the chalkboard to write the number '12' and letters 'D' and 'P' on the board. "Ten girls in ten months," he sighed, "all sixteen years of age — have disappeared on the night of a full moon — hence the curfew you all now have."

"If that's the case, does that mean someone else will go missing?" Melanie Ross asked from the middle of the room. A surge of whispers swirled around the class as she added: "There's supposed to be another full moon tonight."

"With your curfew and the heightened police presence in the area, you should be safe." He reassured us, but it didn't bring me much comfort. "But while we're talking about it, let's think about the events of this past year: ten girls from four different high schools vanish without a trace during similar time frames. What do you think happened, and what *will* happen if this continues?"

"If the disappearances are following a pattern, then there should be a twelfth princess; and then maybe whoever's behind it will stop." I interjected, and I could feel all of their eyes on me again. I didn't understand until I looked to

Mr. Thompson, and my heart sank when he had the same expression on his face.

"You mean eleven—eleven princesses." He corrected me, watching me cautiously—as if I would shatter if I weren't handled correctly. I swallowed, remembering what I had said. To the rest of the world, Heather was dead; but in the labyrinth of my mind, there was a door yet to be opened—an answer that hadn't been discovered yet. I just had to find it.

"Right. Eleven."

I slammed my locker door shut and drew in a deep breath, pressing my forehead against the cold hard metal slathered in red paint.

"Do I *want* to know?" I turned my head to steal a glance to my left. Connor was leaning against his locker beside me, his own Letterman jacket sliding off his right shoulder. For someone who had lived in Oklahoma for half of his life, he still had the air of a city boy.

I guess New York was more than just a place.

"Probably not." I told him, sighing. He buried his hands in the pockets of his jeans and looked at the clock overhead.

"We should take off if we want to get to class on time." He was right. The others were already starting to disappear through the doors leading into the classrooms on either side of the hall. We started to make our way up the stairs to the second floor, and a group of juniors crowding the steps forced us closer to the banister.

"How was stage tech?" I looked back at him from over my shoulder.

"Great." He responded from the landing and hurried to catch up with me. "The lighting's almost finished. We just need to work on the ellipsoidal reflectors for the cyc." I paused in the middle of the staircase, unsure of what he had said.

"English, please?" He shook his head at my request and chuckled to himself.

"They're the lights for the background." He explained, and I grinned at him from the top of the stairs.

"Was that so hard?" He smiled and followed me onto the second floor, and we hurried into the room across the hall. Half of the class was still missing; but we were instantly met with a wall of sound: of Adrienne and the other cheerleaders laughing as they sat atop their desks and talked about their mornings, and of the basketball players going over the homework they had finished during practice. The room smelled of peppermint, something I'd grown accustomed to in Ms. Chambers' class. She let us decorate the classroom for every holiday. I stared up at the silver snowflakes hanging from the ceiling and wondered what the room would look like for Arbor Day.

"Connor." I turned when one of the boys called his name. He hesitated, glancing at me for permission; and I let him leave my side. I wove in between the obstacles of people sitting in chairs and sat down, listening to the voices as they continued on. They grew louder as more students came filing in from the hallway, and then there were thirteen of us in the classroom.

"Hey." He had a habit of surprising me. Connor was suddenly sitting to my right, opening up his binder to the World History section. "They just wanted to check their answers for the Chemistry assignment."

We each had our talents. Connor understood science better than anyone I knew, and he wouldn't let me forget it. It wasn't my best subject or my favorite, so study sessions usually ended with my mom baking cookies to cheer me up. But history—history meant more to me than any of the others. To read a name and realize that the person it belonged to really lived and affected the person that I would become— my father always told me the seeds of our future were sown in the past.

Ms. Chambers rose from the chair at her desk when the bell rang.

"Okay, you guys, class has started." With that, the cheerleaders leapt off of their desks to sit in their seats. "I'd like all of you to get in groups of three so you can start reviewing for the final exam for this semester." I hated group assignments. She stood and waited as I looked around desperately. There were thirteen of us. Connor had already been absorbed by the boys in the front of the class, and I was alone.

"Hey, Melissa." It took me a minute to realize that someone was calling my name. But Adrienne was sitting behind me with a smile on her face, beckoning for me to join her. Kris had given her his jacket during passing period, and she wore it over her shoulders like a cape. "You can join us if you want." I stared at her, confused; but she didn't seem to care. "Are you coming?" I nodded silently and turned my chair in her direction, finding myself sitting in a circle with Hannah Wilson and Chloe Miller. They were pretty, just like Adrienne was; but Hannah's raven black hair made Adrienne's strawberry blonde ponytail pale in comparison. I could feel the blood rush to my face as I blushed, feeling out of place. I was the only one not wearing a cheerleader's uniform.

"What—" My voice cracked, and I cleared my throat. "What did you want to study first?" I started to reach for the textbook lying on my desk, stopping when I caught them staring at me. "Wh—" I wanted to ask them why, but their gazes shifted to something behind me; and I turned to see what it was.

Ms. Chambers was taking attendance.

"I don't know why she bothers." Chloe's wispy voice said sadly. I still wondered how someone so soft-spoken had made the cheerleading squad.

"Maybe she thinks they'll come back." I only realized once I'd said it that it sounded crazy.

"They're not coming back." Adrienne responded, sighing. "For all we know, Becca, Willow, and Val are long gone with the rest of them." She played with her fingers in her lap as she spoke, and I couldn't help but look down myself. It was the first time I'd heard her say anything like that. It didn't make sense—almost made me angry. How could she give up on her friends? How could anyone?

"If they don't catch him, it could be one of us next." Hannah whispered.

"It's like we're waiting in line." Chloe murmured to herself, but it was just loud enough to reach my ears; and I couldn't keep myself from shuddering at the thought of it.

We were all just waiting to disappear— fade away and never be heard from again. And when we did, who'd remember us then? I didn't want to be forgotten—swept away into the void. And I wouldn't let that happen to Heather either.

Chapter Two

What Was Left in the Woods

Screams and bright lights. It was all I could hear — all I could see. I was one in a crowd of hundreds of people, fighting to catch a glimpse of the commotion on the floor. I shouted Connor's name when I finally saw him; and he turned his head in my direction, failing in his attempt to find me in the stands.

"Connor!" I called his name again and stood on my toes, waving my hand over my head so he could see. He smiled when he caught sight of me and stopped to return the gesture.

"Reilly! Get over there!" My ears were suddenly assaulted by the hoarseness of Coach Fields' voice, and I watched as Connor made a face and sprinted away.

"Look what you did. You got him in

trouble." My mother leaned closer to me so I could hear.

"You don't stop and wave in the middle of a game! Fifty laps!" My father spoke with the Southern accent we all knew too well.

The septuagenarian had proven to be a near-immortal fixture at Locust Grove High—the constant center of urban legends and memories for the past two or three generations of students who walked its halls. My father had done so once—and told a great deal of those stories himself.

I looked up at the clock on the scoreboard as it counted down from two minutes and then to the numbers in red lights above it. It was the second half of the game, and we were behind.

"This doesn't look good." I breathed, nervous. Losing the first game wouldn't be a great way to start the season.

"Hold on, now." My father began, and I glanced at him before looking on in apprehension. "A lot can happen in two minutes." I silently shook my head, not really sure if I believed him. One of the boys from the opposing team made another basket, and the score under the word 'Away' changed from fifty-nine to sixty-one. The referee tossed the ball to Kris, and he stood out of bounds to pass it on to another teammate.

"I don—" I never finished. The crowd rose to their feet again as someone raced across the floor with the ball, and I craned my neck to see who it was. Connor stopped in the middle of the court, looking somewhat at a loss. "Go, Connor! Go!" I yelled to him, but I knew that there was no way he could hear me. I saw him take a deep breath—like he always does when he's distressed—and let the ball fly from his hands. I bit my lip as it arced, imagining every possible way it could go wrong.

It could miss and hit the wall or fall short altogether—or it could bounce off the backboard and take him out. And then I thought of him waving to me as the ambulance carried him away.

It was silent as my heart beat out of my chest, pounding in my reddening ears. And then, there was nothing but a swish. I screamed along with the others as the ball fell through the net, so loud I thought I'd lose my voice. And it went from fifty-four to fifty-seven.

"What did I say?" My father shrugged his shoulders as if to say 'I told you so', and I laughed to myself. He was right, but I wouldn't give him the satisfaction of admitting it to his face.

"Look, he's got it again!" My mother exclaimed, and we both returned our attention to the court in time to see Connor pass the ball to Gregory Anderson. "Oh! There he goes!" She almost whispered. The cheerleaders' chants seemed to push him forward as he ran, never stopping as he bounced the ball off the backboard and into the basket for a layup. The clock continued to count down as the other team took the ball across the floor and attempted to make another basket, and I held my breath as it rebounded and found its way into Kris' possession.

Twenty-four.

He darted halfway across the court and was immediately blocked by an opposing player in green and yellow.

Fourteen.

He passed the ball to Connor.

Seven.

Connor's feet left the ground as he threw the ball one more time, and the clock fell to zero. The buzzer went off as the people in the bleachers erupted into a cacophony of cheers, nearly deafening as they flooded the floor. I stood still as they rushed past me, stunned; and I let out a sigh of relief. I raised my head toward the scoreboard and shook my head with a smile. Sixty-two to sixty-one.

I guess a lot can happen in two minutes.

I jostled my way to the center of the crowd where Connor and the other players were, in the middle of all the chaos; and he pulled me into an enthusiastic hug.

"Did you see that?" He panted excitedly, almost as shocked as I was. I nodded.

"I think everyone did." I said, glancing at the sea of red and white surrounding us. It was still so loud, we could barely hear each other.

"Good, 'cause I don't think I'll be able to do that again." He joked, but I could hear the truth in his words.

"Hey, Reilly!" Kris emerged from the crowd and set a hand on Connor's shoulder. "It looks like we've got ourselves a new star player." He remarked, and I could only watch as Connor was whisked away into the noise.

"Melissa!" I grinned expectantly when I heard him call my name before he disappeared. "We're celebrating afterwards." He pointed at me as if it were a demand. "You're coming with me."

A party. It wasn't something I would

have gone to by myself, and he knew it.

I navigated my way back to my parents still sitting in the stands, and they stood at the sight of me.

"Are you ready to go, honey?" My mother asked, slipping her coat on. The nights were getting colder. In the moments before I answered, I debated whether or not I wanted to go with him. He'd bother me about it if I didn't.

"Connor invited me to a party." My mother seemed surprised — or maybe, it was relief I was seeing.

"Oh, okay." She smiled. "Have fun." She embraced me, squeezing a little too tightly. Relief. That's what it was.

"Don't forget the curfew." My father had to remind me. I couldn't imagine staying out past 11:30 anyway.

"I won't." I promised them.

"We'll see you at home." My mother waved goodbye, and she and my father filed out of the gym with the others. The noise died down as the last of them left, and the screams and bright lights were nothing but a memory. I sat down as I waited in the silence, the occasional sound of a basketball bouncing on the floor echoing into the rafters. I looked to the other side of the gym to see where it was coming from to find the coaches putting the equipment back into storage. I watched Coach Fields leave the sack of basketballs in his office and lock the door; and as he turned, he tipped his baseball cap when he saw me.

"Have a good night." He told me, and I nodded in return. "Hurry up, boys! I'm locking up!" He shouted out into the quietness; and almost immediately, the basketball team came dashing out. Connor sprinted to me in his jeans and red sweater, his hair still dripping from the showers.

"Are you ready?" Clearly, he was more excited than I was.

"No." I sighed as I stood, but he merely laughed and draped his arm over my shoulders.

"I expect nothing less."

"Where are we?" I wondered aloud as I stepped out of the car and stared up at the house towering over us. I'd never been in this part of Locust Grove before. All the houses were so big; they reminded me of the school buildings that we had just left behind.

"Ridgewater Lane." I heard the car door slam behind me, and Connor was suddenly standing by my side. "This is Adrienne's house." I gazed at the moonlight that fell over the roof and onto the street, painting the ground in silver light; and Melanie's words found their way into my thoughts.

"...does that mean someone else will go missing?"

He started to move towards it, stopping to look back at me over his shoulder. "Are you coming?" Wordlessly, I followed him up the steps and to the front door. I could tell by the shadows that danced across the frosted glass that dozens of people had arrived before us, and I inhaled in apprehension.

I didn't know if I could handle so many people.

Connor rang the doorbell, but I couldn't imagine anyone hearing it inside. But still, the door swung open; and Chloe Miller's bright green eyes met us on the other side.

"Melissa!" She exclaimed and stepped back to allow us inside. "I'm glad you came." The cold of the night abruptly came to an end when the door closed behind us, and we took a step forward into the living room. In the dim light, I could make out the faces of our peers—

most of them people I was fairly familiar with.

In a small school like ours, nearly everyone knew each other.

"There he is!" And now everyone knew who *he* was. Kris pointed to us from the den, and the crowd of partygoers turned and cheered at our arrival. He gestured for us to join them; but I hesitated, staying behind as Connor obliged. He paused when he realized that I wasn't with him and hurried back to whisper a question.

"Is this too much?" He asked me. "We can always go home if it is."

If anyone deserved something like this, it was Connor.

I forced a smile and pushed him forward.

"Go ahead. I'll be around." I insisted. His eyes lingered for a moment, as if to find the answer I wouldn't tell; but he gave in to my request.

"Okay."

"That was way too close today." Kris continued, speaking loud enough so everyone could hear. "Next time, we've got to hit them harder. They can't come to our home and dominate us like that." The crowd roared in approval. "When they come here, we have to show them who's boss. We have to make sure they remember who we are. Are you with me?" There were a number of shouts in response; and soon, the whole room burst into a chorus of cheers and applause. The music swelled when the sound finally died; and I wandered through the many rooms of the house, meandering around the dancing couples and occasional sinister piece of furniture.

A cold breeze came wafting in from my left and disturbed my hair, and I turned towards it in curiosity. A door leading out onto the terrace was open. I glanced back at the world I couldn't recognize and let myself be taken away into the night. It was quiet and peaceful, something that I needed more than anything at this moment; and in the silence, I leaned over the railing to look out into darkness beyond me.

"I like to come out here, too — when I need time to myself." She was sitting up against the space where the railing met one of the terrace's beams in a rose sequined blouse, a white leather jacket hugging her shoulders. "It's hard, isn't it?" She jumped down from the railing when I didn't answer. "Heather was my best friend, too. When I heard she drowned," she sighed, "I cried for weeks." I stared down at the wooden floor, never taking my eyes off of it.

"She told me where she was going," I

lifted my head to face her, "and I didn't go with her. What kind of person does that make me?"

"Nobody knew what was going to happen." Adrienne took a step towards me. "You can't keep going on like this."

I didn't want to hear it, but she was right.

"Heather may be gone, but *you're* here. You shouldn't live like you're already dead."

I wish I knew how to change, but the thought of leaving Heather's memory behind was unbearable; and I couldn't do it.

"Come back to the cheerleading squad." She pleaded with me. "We miss you. We *need* you. Just don't let this keep you from living your life." I flinched when she reached out to place her hand on my shoulder; and she drew back, almost as if she thought I was afraid of her. I scratched my head, scrambling for the words that had left my mind too soon.

"Um, I—I gotta go." I stuttered, shrugging. "My parents don't want me out too late." It was a terrible excuse, but she let me leave her standing in the blackness. I sauntered into the den, into the dizzying atmosphere of the ever-changing colors of the lights and vibrating speakers. My whole body shuddered with the music, and I had to bite my tongue to keep my teeth from shaking.

Where was he?

Everywhere I turned, I nearly collided with another familiar stranger; but Connor was nowhere to be seen. I scanned the room for him, but it was too difficult to see anything.

"Kris." I paused when I spied him sitting on the couch, and he looked up at the sound of his name.

"Yeah?" He and Thomas Pierson stopped in the middle of their conversation.

"Do you know where Connor is?" I had to ask. If I didn't, it'd probably be another hour until I found him.

Kris blinked at my question.

"Yeah. He's in the kitchen." He gestured to where he'd last seen him. "Do you know where Adrienne went?"

"She's out on the terrace." I turned my head toward the open door behind me. "Thanks." I hurried into the other room to find Connor leaning against the island weighed down with bowls of chips and bottles of soda, struggling to explain how he'd miraculously led the team to the first victory of the season. "Connor?" He smiled and excused himself from the crowd that had congregated around him.

"What's up?" He wanted to know. "Are you having fun?"

I didn't like the idea of telling him I wasn't.

The smile fell from his face when I said nothing, and it was no longer necessary.

"Let's go home." He led the way to the door, speaking before setting his hand on the handle. "What happened?"

"It just…" What could I say? "It just got a little uncomfortable." And suddenly, his blue eyes were as despondent as I must have looked.

"Promise me you'll try." It hurt to see him so heartbroken. I swallowed, instantly feeling guilty.

"I'll be back in a minute." I turned away from him and hurried back into the den, trying and failing in my attempt to dodge a brunette in yellow. "I'm sorry." I apologized, breathless. "I guess I didn't see you."

"Don't worry about it." She shook her head in dismissal and grinned; and I slowed my pace, careful not to run into anybody else. My steps ended abruptly when I wrinkled my forehead in confusion.

I didn't remember seeing her before. But then, there were a few people I didn't recognize here.

I hurried through the den and to the door open to the terrace.

"Adrienne." I panted as I dashed out into the darkness, but I was met with Kris' face instead.

"I guess she went back inside." I sighed as he excused himself and retreated back into the warmth of the house; and I returned to the front door, where Connor was waiting.

"Did you do what you wanted?" I nodded without a word; and he pulled the door open, exposing us to a rush of cold wind as it passed by. He checked his watch as we descended the steps. "So it's 9:27 right now." He said when he reached the car. "Do you mind staying out a little longer?" I eyed him suspiciously from the other side.

"It depends on where we're going..." He chuckled at my words.

"Don't worry. It's not another party." He reassured me. "Who knows? You might actually have some fun." I shook my head, still a little skeptical; but his sarcasm made me smile.

"Fine." I opened the door and slid into my seat; and for a second, I swore I heard him whoop in victory. I fastened my seatbelt and turned to him again, not entirely satisfied with his answer. "Do I get to know where we're going?"

"No." The engine revved as the headlights flickered on. "It's a surprise."

Surprises. I hadn't had the best experience with those lately.

I awoke with a start, with a sudden gasp for air that burned when it filled my lungs. It was only when I came to that I realized it was cold air that I was breathing, and I exhaled again to see a puff of mist escape my lips. It was small and so faint, I could have imagined it; but like a ghost, it was gone.

"Connor—" I turned my head toward the driver's seat to face him, but it was empty. I sat up in alarm, and the Letterman jacket draped over me slid down onto the floor.

Why had he left his jacket behind?

"Connor?" I called his name again, but only silence answered. Groggily, I pushed the car door open and stepped outside, into the few beams of moonlight that found their way through the tree branches; and I looked up at the sky. Clouds were beginning to drift across it, obscuring the stars from view. I circled the car and stole a wary glance over my shoulder when I crushed a twig underneath my foot. A wall of trees lined both sides of the dirt road, the shadows they cast falling over my face. It was quiet—in an unnerving sort of way; and then, I heard the rustle of a handful of leaves scrape over the ground. I whirled around to face whoever it might have been, but there was no one. Footsteps echoed in my ears, and I turned to find myself inches from a figure standing over me. "Very funny, Connor." I rolled my eyes as he frowned.

"You just kill all the fun, don't you?" He reached into the Oldsmobile for his jacket and slipped it on.

"Just yours." I walked past him and toward the sound of water gurgling beyond the trees. "Where are we?" A devilish grin crept its way onto his face.

"Come on. Let me show you." Eagerly, he led me down the road and toward the clearing in the distance. "Do you remember what was on your list?" It took me a second to realize what he was talking about.

"Sure," I finally replied, "Amityville House, Eastern State Penitentiary, Edinburgh Castle, Gettysburg, Myrtles Plantation, the Queen Mary, the Tower of London, Whaley House, the White House, and Winchester House." I had read their names in a list last year, and I hadn't forgotten them. They were places I wanted to visit — or rather, places the three of us wanted to visit.

"You forgot one." He stopped, falling silent when we reached the end of the woods; and I stole a step forward to see why.

There before us stood the rusted skeleton of the Crybaby Bridge, its looming abutments the only remnants of its existence. It seemed almost eerie in the moonlight, the way it hovered over us — in a silence that only death could accomplish. I imagined the woman's screams as her car plunged into the water below, and I shuddered.

"So this is it?" I never thought I'd get the chance to see it.

"Yep." Connor said as he joined me. "You can scratch this one off your list." I started to move towards it, but his hand held me back. "Careful." He warned me. "It's just the frame now."

Right. I almost forgot. Adding myself to

the legend wasn't exactly what I had in mind.

"You know we won't see anything." I remarked, running my hand along the metal railing.

"Because ghosts don't exist?" He quipped, and I found myself shaking my head.

There'd be a plate of cookies in my future if I let him continue.

"No." I responded matter-of-factly. "It's not midnight."

"Speaking of midnight," Connor spoke as he glanced at his watch, "we should be taking off soon if we want to be home by curfew." I sighed.

So soon?

"Just a minute." I whispered, as if it had been to myself; and my fingers began to trace the scratches in the rusted steel.

It was unsettling in a strange way. I couldn't help but wonder where they came from. Some of them looked like broken letters—as if the one who had left them had been trying to send a message. A series of grooves caught my eye, and I peered at them in curiosity. Three letters—spelling a single word.

"Lyn." I said it aloud.

"What?" I didn't know that he had heard me.

"There's a word—or a name carved into the railing." I stuttered, unable to describe it to him.

"Really?" I turned, nearly startled out of my wits when I found him standing behind me. "What does it say?"

I wish I knew.

"L...y...n." I looked up at him, unsure of what it meant.

A strange sensation suddenly gripped my hand, and I stared down at it in alarm. Water. But the way it sparkled in the moonlight seemed strange—unnatural even—and for a moment, it merely sat there, as if that was where it belonged. Another drop of rain splashed onto the railing beside my fingers, and I pulled my hand back as more kept falling. I gazed up at the clouds as the sky was torn open; and lightning electrified the darkened world that we were standing in, thunder shattering the silence.

"We should go." He breathed, and I stole one last glance over my shoulder at the abandoned bridge as he grasped my hand and pulled me away. And for a second, I saw a blue light burning in the distance.

Quietly, I unlocked my front door and stepped inside. I sighed in relief as warm air instantly surrounded me and turned to wave goodbye as Connor drove away and out of sight. The clock mounted on the wall ticked behind me, and I looked up at it in apprehension.

11:52.

Maybe they were asleep. It wasn't likely, but I could hope.

"Melissa?" And suddenly, that hope was dashed to pieces. My mother hurried to me; and before I could breathe, I was bombarded with a million questions. "Where have you been?" She laid her hands on my shoulders, drawing them back when she saw that my clothes were soaked through. "How did you get so wet? I didn't hear anything about it raining."

"It did in Kellyville." I trudged past her, my soggy shoes squishing across the carpet; and she followed me, wrinkling her forehead in confusion.

"Kellyville's an hour away. What were

you doing there?" It was a pretty good question.

I stopped beside the couch to shed my coat and dropped it on one of the cushions.

"We went to Crybaby Bridge." I told her; and I saw her eyes widen, even if it only lasted a millisecond. "Connor thought it would be fun."

If that made it better.

"Did you—have fun?" She asked me, and what I had seen in her eyes had found its way into her voice. Worry? Or fear?

"Yeah." I nodded, still watching her; and she smiled. That didn't happen very often.

"I'm glad you made it home okay." She wrapped her arms around me in an embrace and whispered. "Now, get some sleep. You've got a long day tomorrow." She let go, and I lifted my jacket up from the couch on my way to the stairs. "Melissa."

"Yeah, Mom?" I paused on the landing; and in the darkness, the moonlight bled through the windows and onto her face.

"Don't go there again." I blinked at her request, but I could tell that she was serious.

"Okay." I swallowed and stood there for a moment, questions of my own running through my head. But I buried them—and stepped out of the light and into the shadows.

Chapter Three

Orion

"You should have seen the look on her face." I started as we walked through the cafeteria and to our table in the corner. There, we could see the rest of the student body in its entirety — watch them as if they were on the other side of a TV screen. It was always the same: Kris would be sitting with Thomas and Gregory, reliving the final moments of their victory in the previous night's game; and Adrienne and her friends would be late to lunch after going over their cheer routines in the gym.

But today was different. I couldn't describe it, but there was something — something very wrong.

"It's like I told her I killed you and buried you in the backyard." I said, prying open the carton of apple juice with my fingernails. I looked up at Connor and then to the tray of food he hadn't touched. "What? You're not hungry?"

"Not anymore." He remarked as he dropped a tater tot from his fingers, and it rolled back and forth in the Styrofoam plate. I shrugged and stole it from him, popping it into my mouth. The soft filling burst behind my lips when my teeth crushed the crunchy coating, and the taste of salt and pepper drove me towards my apple juice. "Did she ground you?" He wanted to know.

"No." I shook my head. "She *wants* me to get out more. If she were going to punish me, that's the last thing she would do." He chuckled a little.

"Yeah, I guess you're right." His head perked up as a thought occurred to him, and I eyed him suspiciously.

What was he thinking?

"Hey, can I practice my moves on you?" I paused, confused; and he held up a tater tot to clarify.

Oh – for basketball.

"Shoot." I told him, and he tossed the first. I opened my mouth to catch it, but it hit my forehead instead and tumbled onto the table. "That was terrible!" I exclaimed, wiping the grease from my face with the back of my hand.

"Let me do it again." He insisted, and I gave in. Another flew up into the air; and this time, I caught it. "Yes!" He held up his hand for a high five, our palms meeting in a smack when I obliged.

"Hey." I lowered my hand at the sound of his voice. Kris was suddenly sitting at our table.

"Hi, Kris. What's up?" I asked him, but something told me I already knew. The veins in his eyes were as red as fire, revealing how little sleep he had gotten the night before. He ran his fingers through his dark hair and sighed, trying to take a deep breath and failing. I knew what he was going to ask, and my heart beat out of my chest and into my throat as I waited.

I wanted to close my eyes and count to ten, in the blind hope that all of this was just a nightmare—and wake up to the sound of Connor talking to my father about fishing in the spring—and Heather sharing Mrs. Harrison's croissants with my mother. But January was gone, and so was any thought that it could ever be the way that it was before.

"Have you seen Adrienne?" Connor silently shook his head across from me in response.

"Not since last night." I told him and watched him fall apart in front of me.

I knew that look. He thought she was dead.

"Have you asked Chloe or Hannah? They were at the party, right? They probably saw her after we left." I tried to reason with myself, but what wasn't being said was just enough to say it all.

"I did. They—they didn't see her." He stuttered. "When you talked to her, did she say anything about leaving the party?"

"No. She just wanted a little time to herself." Kris sighed at my answer, and I tried my best to reassure him. "Maybe she stayed home or had a late doctor's appointment."

It was worth a try.

He nodded in his attempt to believe it and somberly rose to his feet.

"Thanks, you guys." And he was gone. I stared down at my plate and took a deep breath of my own.

"It's not fair." I looked up at Connor as he stole a glance over his shoulder and at Kris sitting with the rest of the basketball team. "People are going missing, and we can't do anything about it."

"Connor." I could feel my stomach twisting inside me as the puzzle in my mind came together, and the thought of it made my lungs as heavy as a heap of stones. He turned his head when I called his name, and I could tell by his reaction that he recognized the horror in my eyes. "If no one saw Adrienne after we left," the words felt cold and terrifying on my tongue, "then whoever took her was at the party last night."

The shrill tone of the school bell rang in my ears long after it had stopped, and a hundred bodies brushed past me as I fought my way through the hall and to the doors leading out into the open air. My skin prickled as a sharp breeze gathered up my hair and sent it flying all around me, and I struggled to keep it close to my reddening ears.

"It's the ranch today, right?" Connor laid his hand on my shoulder to announce himself.

"Yeah." I answered. "I have to take an extra shift for breaking curfew."

It didn't really bother me that much. I

liked working with the horses at my parents' ranch. But if I told them that, they wouldn't have chosen it for my punishment.

"Okay." He stopped when we reached the edge of the parking lot. "Stay here. I'll get the car." He breathed before crossing the sea of asphalt without me. I stood at the edge of the sidewalk and waited as students passed me by, and I held my arms tightly to keep myself warm. I gazed down at my shadow in the sunlight, blinking when I found myself looking at two instead of one. I took my eyes off of them, only to realize that someone was standing beside me.

Light brown wavy locks fell past her shoulders and onto the orchid jacket she wore over a white flowery blouse. I squinted at her, silently running through the faces that passed me every day at school; but she wasn't in them. And then I remembered.

"You were at the party last night." I didn't realize that I had spoken until she turned in my direction.

"Oh." She must have recognized me. "Hi. I'm Dorothy." She introduced herself. "Nice to meet you."

"My name's Melissa—I don't think I've seen you around before." I gestured to the school building behind us.

"Just moved here from Massachusetts." She explained, shrugging her shoulders and taking in the unfamiliar world around her. "It's...kind of a big change." She chuckled. "But I think I can handle it."

I went back and forth in my head debating whether or not I should tell her—tell her that the girl she met the night before, the girl with the long blonde hair and bright blue eyes, was gone.

A silver truck suddenly pulled up in front of us, prompting Dorothy into motion.

"That's my brother." She turned to face me before throwing open the door and climbing inside.

"Wait." I called out to her and she kept the door open to listen. "How old are you?" I'm sure it seemed like a strange question, but she smiled in response.

"Seventeen." The word sent a wave of relief flooding over me. "And you?"

"Almost sixteen." I grinned as I told her, hiding the apprehension that came with the number.

I'd be sixteen in three weeks, and then what would happen?

"Cool. I'll see you around." She closed the car door, and I watched the curly-haired driver as he turned the wheel and sped away. The loud burst of a horn startled me, and I looked down to see Connor waving to me from the driver's seat of his Oldsmobile.

"Who was that?" He waited for me to buckle my seatbelt before he asked.

"New girl at school." I leaned my head against the window as I held my knuckles to my lips. "I bumped into her at the party last night."

"She doesn't know?" It was silent for a moment, the quietness only broken when he turned the key in the ignition.

"No."

"What's on your mind?" Connor glanced at me from the driver's seat. The town of Salina and Hudson Lake were far behind us; and in the distance, I could see the city of Pryor on the horizon.

"How do twelve girls just disappear in a place where there hasn't been a murder for years?" Thinking about it now, it seemed so strange. "And why hasn't anyone found their bodies yet?"

"Maybe there aren't any bodies to be found." I looked up at him as he shrugged his shoulders. "Maybe he's not killing them." I shuddered at the thought of what whoever 'he' was could have been doing.

I'm sure wherever Adrienne was, she wished she was dead.

"Does your mom know anything?" I asked him. "She still works at the newspaper, doesn't she?"

"She knows as much as we do." I sighed at his words. "But we can drop by on Saturday if you want." He replied as we slowly passed underneath the sign of rusted metal that hung above us. The words 'Moonwater Ranch' marked the entrance, a crescent moon in place of one of the o's. The sound of children laughing and hooves cantering up the trail grew louder as we neared the end of the road, and rows of vehicles with dusty tires filled the unpaved parking lot.

"Sounds like a plan." I unbuckled my seatbelt when he stopped by the curb and stepped out of the car, waving goodbye. "I'll see you tomorrow." He nodded with a smile and drove away, leaving me standing by the doors.

Orion

"Have any of you ever wondered what the stars are like?" I opened up one of the doors and stepped inside, immediately moving to the corner of the room at the sound of my mother's voice. What looked like a dozen children sat on cushions on the floor, gazing up at her in wonder; and I smiled to myself, remembering when I did the same. "Some people say that they're just balls of light, but others say that they're people like you and me." She began, and I leaned against the wall and listened. "Boys, raise your hands." As soon as she spoke, seven hands eagerly shot up into the air. "Imagine a couple of boys just like you were playing with sticks and stones every day. Now, their mothers didn't like it; but every time they told them to stop, those boys would run off to do just that. So when they came home for dinner one day, their mothers decided to give them the stones to eat instead. The boys didn't like that at all, so they ran away and started dancing."

"Dancing?" One boy interjected, screwing up his face in confusion.

"That's right. But this dance wasn't any ordinary dance." She lowered her voice as if she were sharing a secret. "This dance made them fly." I grinned when her audience gasped in awe, suddenly captivated. "When their mothers went out to look for them, they were already too high up for them to reach — all except one. But when that little boy reached the ground, he turned into great big pine tree." She opened up her arms to show its stature.

"Was it as tall as my daddy?" A child with pigtails asked her, her voice small and wispy. My mother's eyes sparkled when she looked into the little girl's face.

"The tallest." Her response was met with a timid giggle. "But the other boys," she returned her attention to the rest of the children, "they rose higher and higher until they reached the sky; and there, they became six bright shining stars. So the next time you look up at the night sky, know that somewhere up there, there are boys playing their favorite game." She glanced up as a shadow darkened the opposite doorway. My father. Despite his heavy coat and mittens, he still managed to look like a cowboy.

"All right, kids. Who wants to ride some horses?" He clapped his hands; and they rose to their feet, racing to swarm around him. I watched them disappear through the doorway and into the corral.

"I don't remember that story." I remarked, taking a step forward.

"That's because you were always interested in those other ones." She answered me as she stood and folded the blanket that had been in her lap. "What were their names: Zeus and Pyrenees and the one with the snakes on top of her head?"

At least she got one.

"Okay. You've made your point." I relieved her of the blanket and set it down on her chair. "What did you want me to do while I'm here?" She placed her hands on her hips and sighed.

"Well, the stables need mucking out."

"I'll get right on it." I replied and started to move towards the door.

"Not so fast." She called out to me; and I stopped, whirling around to face her. "You're closing tonight."

"Okay." I swallowed.

They never had me lock up the business by myself.

She passed by me, patting me on the back as she slipped out of the room.

"Make sure you're home on time."

The sunlight that seeped through the open windows and into the stables began to fade as the day came to an end. The children that had once roamed the ranch were long gone, and the only sound that accompanied me was the crunch of the shavings underneath my boots. I took a step back to assess what I had done and sighed, exhausted. It took two hours, but I was finished.

"Hey, Melissa." I looked up at the sound of my name. Mason Whitaker, one of the ranch hands, poked his head through the doorway.

"Can I bring them in, now?" He rubbed his gloved hands together in an attempt to keep them warm.

"Sure." I leaned the pitchfork up against the nearest beam and dusted off my own, pulling the gloves away from my fingers as the first of twelve horses came trotting in.

"Your parents asked me to drive you home." He said as he led the horse into the third stall on my right. I nodded my head slowly, a little perplexed.

"Don't you live in Claremore?" I started. "My house is kind of out of the way."

Forty miles, actually.

"They wanted to make sure that you got

home all right." He told me.

But still, I couldn't help but feel terrible for him.

"I could always walk." I jokingly suggested, sprinting after him to take the reins of a palomino. He laughed and glanced back at me from over his shoulder before leading a golden champagne horse into her stall.

"Not a chance." He answered and swung the door into place. "Have you locked the front doors yet?" I shook my head. "If you finish bringing the others in, I'll go ahead and do that." He offered, and I couldn't say no.

"Thanks Mason." I called after him, and he turned to tip his hat with a smile. And then I was standing in the silence once again. I closed the palomino's stall door and stared at the nameplate with fondness.

Apollo

My father had let me name the horses when I was seven. Even then, the thought of gods and goddesses enchanted me.

I let the rest of the pantheon into the stables, a milky white horse as light as the moon the last of them. She whinnied softly just as I began to close her into her stall, and I pushed it open to lay a hand on her muzzle.

"What's wrong, Artemis?" I whispered, wishing she could tell me. The slight rustle of the shavings being disturbed underfoot caught my attention; and I whirled toward it, expecting to see Mason returning from the front of the ranch. But there was nothing. "Mason?" I shouted his name, but he didn't respond. "Mason." When he didn't answer the second time, I inched slowly out of the stall and stepped backwards towards the back of the stables. My father kept a rifle on the back wall in case a coyote came around. I reached for it, gripping it close as if merely holding it would keep me safe. It wasn't a full moon — that night had already passed; but I wasn't about to take any chances. "I don't like shooting animals, but I've got no problem with people!" I yelled as I pointed the barrel at the door. For seconds, I waited — in the agony of not knowing what might come through the door.

If it were a coyote, at least I'd have a chance. I could fire a few rounds into the ground to scare it off. But people — people were a lot more dangerous.

Crunch after crunch came, with no words to announce whomever they belonged to. I cocked the rifle as my heart began to beat into my throat, and the click that signaled that I wasn't afraid to shoot echoed into the darkness.

"I mean business!" I yelled; and suddenly, a shadow darted across the floor and slowly bled into the stables. The first thing I saw was a cowboy hat; and immediately, I thought that it was Mason. But as the figure drew closer, I knew that it wasn't. A boy — probably no older than eighteen — cautiously stole a step forward with his hands over his head. His brown eyes were open wide, as if he was surprised to see the gun in my hands. He glanced down at it, and then back to rest his stare at my face.

"Please, don't shoot." He said; and for a moment, I forgot where I was.

There was something about him — something that made me smile. But when he grinned in return, it fell from my face; and I remembered what I was holding.

"We're closed." I lowered the rifle away from his head, still clutching it by my side.

"Were you really going to shoot me?" He brought his hands down in relief.

"Maybe." No, I wasn't. "Depends on what you were looking for when you came here." Stealing equipment — or even horses — definitely wasn't uncommon.

"My brothers wanted to sneak back here to see the horses. That's all." He turned to make a gesture to something in the darkness, and two little boys emerged from the shadows. They were young, maybe younger than I was when my father took over the ranch from my grandfather; and unlike their brother, their eyes lit up at the sight of the weapon in my hand. I blinked, not expecting to see a pair of the same face staring back at me. I smiled at their expressions of awe when they saw the horses towering over them; and in them, I saw the same excitement that Heather and Connor shared when they came with me to the ranch for the first time.

"Oh—um…" I stuttered and un-cocked the rifle, placing it back onto the wall as Mason came trudging in with the keys in hand. "How about we do something better? Mason, would you mind saddling up Hermes and Artemis for our guests?" He flashed me a puzzled look, but eventually gave in to my request.

"C'mon, kids." With the reins of both horses in his grip, he led the way back into the corral; and the twins leapt after him, unable to contain themselves.

"That sure was nice of you." The boy in the cowboy hat remarked. "Thanks."

"Don't mention it." I sighed as I locked up Artemis' stall.

"That was somethin' brave — pulling that gun on me." He continued, and I eyed him suspiciously.

Where was he going with this?

"What if I had one?" I smirked as I walked past him and into the frigid night air.

"You'd be on the ground." That was the truth.

"My name's Caleb, by the way." He removed his hat and held it to his chest as he followed me, unrelenting.

"I'm Melissa." I turned my head to glance at him midstride; and in the starlight, I saw him more clearly. His black hair stopped at his shoulders, his chestnut complexion matching mine. With his hat, he managed to tower over me by several inches; and he had a face that equaled his charm.

"Melissa — that's a nice name." I stopped at his words and stared at him incredulously.

"You do realize you just broke into my parents' business, right?" There was that smile again.

"Is it really breakin' in if the door was unlocked?" He shrugged, and I crossed my arms. "I get it. I'm sorry." He apologized. "They just don't get to see horses up close too often." As if to reinforce his explanation, the two boys began to laugh on the other side. I whirled away from him and returned my attention to the two horses strolling towards us. We waved as they passed us by, the sound of cantering hooves quickly fading into silence. "Some night, huh?" He buried his hands in his pockets as he spoke. "You can see all the stars." I gazed up at the sky with him and wondered if the stars were watching us too.

If I could only know what the stars have seen—know every secret hidden in the shadows of the night—would I know what happened to Adrienne? Or even Heather?

But when I glanced at him staring at the world above us, that lingering heartache ceased to exist.

"See—" I started, pointing up at the sky; but he had already done the same.

"See that?" And I let him continue. "Those three stars in a line—that's Orion's Belt."

"The Hunter…" I whispered, grinning to myself. "He's my favorite."

"That makes sense." He chuckled, and I turned to him in alarm.

"Why?" He smirked, setting his gaze once again on the stars.

"He loved the moon." He simply said.

Was it my name that he was referring to? Or did he know that Artemis was mine?

"And she loved him." It felt strange, knowing someone who appreciated it as much as I did; but reality tore the smile from my face, and I frowned. Suddenly, I saw her holding him in her arms, knowing that she had been the one that had taken his life.

"Until he died." I took a deep breath to try to stop the tears that inevitably came, and I scrambled to wipe them away. It wasn't Orion that I wept for — but for someone else entirely.

"Hey." I retreated away from him when he saw how upset I'd become. "Are you all right?" I ran my fingers through my hair with a sigh.

"I'll survive." I turned and made my way back to the stables.

"Wait." I stopped to look back at him, expecting another clever remark. But there was none. "Whatever you're goin' through," he began, his voice shaking in the cold, "I've got a feeling I understand." I nodded my head, if only to be polite, and smiled sadly.

No, he didn't.

Chapter Four

Where Memories are Buried

"*After sixty hours, sixteen-year-old Adrienne Shelley has yet to be found. She was last seen in her home Wednesday night during what is described as a celebration of the local high school's victory in a basketball game. Students who attended the party have given accounts of seeing Shelley in her backyard only moments before her disappearance. This has been the eleventh in a series of disappearances taking place in a span of nearly a year. In addition to Ms. Shelley, the authorities are investigating the disappearances of Stephanie Steinbeck, Kerri Redmouth, Eva Flores, Gabrielle Sakoeka, Jennifer Garcia, Jasmine Berryhill, Valerie Swahl, Iliana Lopez, Rebecca Lawrence, and Willow Grey Eyes.*"

The anchorwoman's words echoed in my ears as

I hurried down the stairs, skipping every other step until my feet reached the hardwood floor. My father turned down the volume and stood when I entered the living room, and I slowed when I saw the look on his face.

"What's wrong?" I asked him, knowing full well what it was. I glanced at the television screen and at Adrienne's smiling face forever immortalized in the pictures her parents had given the police, and I understood. "You know it happened at the party…" I sighed as I slipped my jacket over my shoulders.

"Come here." He gestured for me to come closer, and he pulled me into a hug when I finally did. "I'm just glad you're safe." Tears began to fill my eyes when I realized that Adrienne's parents would never know that feeling again. The doorbell rang, coming to my rescue; and I let go to answer the door.

"That's Connor." I said before pulling it open. Sure enough, he was standing on the other side.

"Hey. Are you ready for our trip to Pryor?" He stepped inside, rubbing his hands together as he breathed on them for warmth.

"What about breakfast?" My mother interjected from the kitchen; and within seconds, she had joined us in the living room, still drying off a plate in her hands with a towel.

"Mom," I paused, surprised that she had forgotten, "it's Saturday." For a moment, it was silent; and then she nodded.

"That's right." She reached out to wrap her arms around me and squeezed me tightly. "Stay safe." I nodded at her words and followed Connor out into the open.

"The usual place?" He exhaled as he stepped onto the sidewalk, glancing back at me for an answer.

"The usual place."

It wasn't far—it only took a few minutes; but the drive to Cedar Crest Lake seemed to last forever. I don't know why we did it—to torture ourselves? No. I think it was more complicated than that. That place—it used to mean something different; but now, as I walked toward the edge of the water, each step was more interminable than the next.

"It's weird, isn't it?"

I turned at the sound of a voice I knew too well; and behind me, I saw myself, sitting cross-legged underneath an old birch tree.

"What's weird?" Heather turned to face me from her spot on Connor's blanket, staring at me with her light green eyes.

"That we're having a picnic in the snow?" Connor quipped as he opened up the wooden basket.

"No." I shook my head at his remark. "We've been coming here for years – this is literally the place that we met," I paused, thinking about it myself, "and we've never been over there." I stared out at the piece of land that seemed to float on the surface of the water, the ground unseen by most shrouded in a curtain of trees. Connor cocked his head to side at the thought of it.

"Huh…I guess you're right." He reached into the picnic basket for another item and retrieved a plastic container, holding it up to his face to see what was inside. "Really?" He looked to Heather, knowing she had been the culprit. "More cake?" Heather inched closer to me and threw her arm over my shoulders.

"C'mon, Melissa just turned fifteen. She deserves to celebrate all week." She insisted; and Connor sighed, muttering under his breath.

"This is what I get for having girls for best friends." But Heather heard him.

"Oh please, you love us." She exclaimed,

smiling. *And then she turned to me, her fiery red hair whipping around her face as she did. "Let's do it." She whispered, as if she were telling me a secret. I could only stare at her, unsure of what she meant. "Let's go there." She laughed at my silence. "All of us," she said louder, so even Connor could hear, "we should go and see what's there."*

"It'll be our own little adventure." I grinned and imagined the three of us claiming the island as our own — having something to run away to when the rest of the world became too much.

"Someday..." He glanced at the two of us with a smile, and I responded with one of my own before gazing at the island once again.

"Maybe."

Heather Harrison was better than all of us. She looked at the world and saw something more. She looked at Cedar Crest and saw the mystery. Me? I never saw it — not until I started looking. And even then, all I saw was her footprints — the ones she didn't even know she left behind.

"What if she made it?" It didn't make any sense; but I needed something to hold on to — however miniscule it was.

"Even if she did — it's been eleven months." I didn't even realize that he was standing beside me. "She would have found a way back by now." I looked up at him, lowering my eyes when he returned my gaze.

"What if she didn't want to?" I remembered staring at the ivory coffin encumbered with a mass of daffodils and lilacs—one for every heart that loved her—knowing that it was empty. In some sick way, it gave me hope. It still did. But after nearly a year, that thing with feathers started to burn; and I knew it was only a matter of time before it fell from the sky.

"There's only one way to find out." He took a step forward towards the water, and I leapt in his way in an attempt to keep him back.

"Wait, what are you doing?" I asked him nervously; but he merely smiled, blue eyes gleaming. He cupped his hands around his mouth and shouted loudly.

"Is anybody out there?" He called out into the clearing, his voice carrying across the crystalline surface of the water and into the trees of the island in the distance. We waited—for what felt like an eternity, we waited. But there was only silence in return. I sighed quietly to myself; and Connor turned, sensing my disappointment. "I'm sorry." He didn't have to apologize. It wasn't his fault. "C'mon." He draped his arm over my shoulders, and we began to make our way down the trail and into the sudden explosion of civilization at the edge of the woods. "We've got work to do."

"Wait." We both turned, surprised that someone had answered at all. And out of the rows of trees that lined the dirt path walked a face I'd missed.

"Hi..." There wasn't much else that I could say. Matthew Brown had lost just as much as I had; and we'd both disappeared into ourselves—in our own way.

"How long have you been standing here?" Connor asked him.

"A while..." He cleared his throat as he continued, stuttering. "I—I know the three of you used to come here." I nodded sadly.

"Yeah...we did." It was quiet for a moment as we stared at each other, and tears suddenly filled his eyes.

"I thought maybe, if I came here, it wouldn't be so hard." His voice trembled as he spoke, and he ran his hands through his hair before burying them in his pockets. "But I was wrong." I hurried to him as he crumbled before me and wrapped my arms around him in an embrace as he wept into my shoulder.

"If she's out there, I'll find her." I swore to him. "I promise. I'll find her."

I looked out the window and at the clouds that hid the sky and strangled the sun, the buildings we passed by just tall enough to obscure the street signs standing on the corners. Nothing had changed — not really — except the whitewashed walls of each building seemed to move, fluttering in the gentle wind that blew past. I peered at them and saw that they were made of faces — the carefree smiles of eleven girls that seemed so sad now. They were gone, and all that was left were those pictures…those smiles. Connor's green Oldsmobile turned the corner onto Adair Street and rolled past the front of Mrs. Harrison's restaurant, and I watched as she swept a handful of crumpled leaves from the sidewalk.

"Here we are." He breathed when we stopped in a parking lot across the street from an antique shop, and the whir of the engine died when he took the key out of the ignition. I unbuckled my seatbelt and stepped outside, gazing up at the little white building a few yards away.

"What do you expect to find here?" I

asked, wanting to know.

"I'm really not sure." He replied after slamming the car door shut. "A connection—a clue, maybe? It's a pretty quiet town. If something like this has happened before, it's bound to have been in the papers."

"What makes you think it's happened before?" I inquired as we hurried onto the sidewalk and to the glass doors, and he paused before going inside.

"You know the stage tech teacher—Rebecca's grandfather—Mr. Lawrence?" I nodded without a word and let him continue. "He said something in class yesterday. It was weird—like he'd been through this before." He responded and pulled one of them open. A woman looked up at us from her desk in the front and smiled when she recognized our faces.

"Hi, Mrs. Reilly." I said as I leaned up against the counter, letting my fingers rest on the surface.

"Hey, Connor...Melissa—I didn't know you'd be coming so early." She tucked a lock of her mane of golden hair behind her ear and away from her emerald green eyes with her left hand; and in that moment, I spied the diamond ring that still clung to her finger. I never saw her without it—even though the man that gave it to her was long gone. He didn't leave them…at least, not willingly. But as New York rebuilt itself from the ashes, so did she—just somewhere far far away.

"We just wanted to get as much research done as possible." He shrugged, and she rose from her seat gripping a baby blue lanyard.

"Okay. Follow me." She grinned and led us through the door behind her and into a cluttered room filled with racks and shelves heavy with plastic boxes. It was dark—ominous almost—until she flipped the switch on the wall and let a sudden burst of fluorescent light flood the room. The air smelled of dust and old paper and ink, and I sneezed when I made the mistake of inhaling too deeply.

"Bless you!" She turned to face me, and I saw how concerned she was. "I hope you're not catching the flu—"

"It's just a little dusty." I explained, pushing my long black hair away from my face.

"I'm sure." She agreed and placed her hands on her hips. "Not too many people go back here besides me. But," she continued as she disappeared down one of the aisles to retrieve a box from a shelf, "oddly enough, you are the second to ask about looking into the archives for a school project." She placed it in Connor's arms;

and by the way he gasped in surprise, it must have been heavier than he thought. "Here are all of the papers from 1936 to start. You're just writing a report on the history of the city, right?"

"Wait." I blinked, taken off guard. "You said someone else asked about the archives?" The thought puzzled me. "Did they say what they were looking for?"

"The same thing as you—he just wanted to take a look at some of the editions from the 1940s and on." Mrs. Reilly remarked, nonchalant.

"He?" Connor repeated.

"Yeah—probably a year or two older than you, dark skin, black hair, very sweet. Is he in your World History class?" I paused, confused.

There was no project—so who had beaten us to the newspaper archives?

"Um...yeah, he must be." I didn't dare to deny it, even if it wasn't true. If she knew what we were *really* doing—that wouldn't go over very well.

"Okay, well, I've got to get back to work; but if you're looking for something specific, the newspapers are organized by year and the shelves are by decade." She remarked before making her way towards the door. "I'll be in the front if you need me." And then, she was gone.

"How are we supposed to find anything in here?" I wondered aloud. "There have to be at least seventy boxes." Connor set the container down on the floor and situated himself on his knees, blowing a layer of dust from its surface.

"Well, I guess we'd better get started."

I yawned as I leafed through the front pages of each newspaper, rubbing the strained eyes that began to fill with tears. Six white boxes sat around me; and I could only skim through each one, drowning in a sea of paper. A soft buzz suddenly accompanied the ticking of the clock hanging on the wall, and I looked up at the ceiling to see that the lights were flickering.

"Have you found anything yet?" Connor asked me two aisles away.

"Nothing so far." I called to him through the gaps in the metal racks. It was difficult, but I could see him with boxes marked from 1972 to 1976. He'd made less progress than I had. "Most of them are covering the soldiers that left the town during World War II. I think I'm going to go ahead and skip to the fifties. They probably have less to say about the Cold War and more about what was going on locally." In the silence, I heard him sigh.

"I really hate history. So many names— dates." He exclaimed, the exasperation present in his voice.

"That's why you have me." I answered, smiling. I lifted the lid from another container and set it beside me, not bothering to look at the year in which its contents had been published. I started to flip through the newspapers that lay inside, trying hard to ignore my own frustration.

How much longer would this take?

"Connor." I stopped; and then, I had my answer.

"Yeah?" He poked his head into my aisle to listen. I pulled the paper out from between the others and held it to my eyes with trembling fingers.

"It's titled 'Young Teen Disappears: Drowning or Foul Play?'" I spoke the words aloud, suddenly feeling Connor staring over my shoulder.

"In what year was it published?" He inquired, curious. I squinted my eyes at the date printed at the top of the page.

"June 2, 1950." I continued reading. "On May 31st, coincidentally the night of an astronomical phenomenon, sixteen-year-old April Lawson disappeared from Ce—" I stuttered, not sure if I could continue.

"What is it?" I was almost afraid to answer.

"'April Lawson disappeared from Cedar Crest Lake while reportedly swimming with her younger sister, Abigail. Abigail, the only other person present at the lake when April went missing, claims to have seen a flash of lightning before realizing that her sister was no longer with her—a strange occurrence at this time of year if it is proven to be true. The authorities will be investigating further into this case to determine whether April Lawson simply drowned or if she fell victim to an act of malice.'" I lowered the newspaper from my face slowly, as if merely taking the time would restore my memories of the names.

I knew I'd heard them before, but where—that was the question.

"I found something else." He grunted as he squeezed past a couple of boxes to join me. "I'm not sure you're going to like it."

"Why?" I asked him, leaning closer to see the paper he clutched in his hands.

"It's about another disappearance," he hesitated before handing it to me, "from 1976."

"Okay." Why was he acting like that? What could be so terrible that he wasn't certain if he wanted me to know?

"Apparently, another girl went missing from Cedar Crest in the seventies. Only this time, it was from her house. The police thought that the widower the family brought onto their property to stay and work as a handyman was behind it, but they couldn't prove anything." I glanced at him, wary as I took it.

"Chelsea Banneker..." I skimmed over the words, halting at the picture of the Banneker family standing in front of a house that looked all too familiar. But it was a face—the face of the widower beside them that gave me pause—made my heart sink into my stomach. I looked to Connor sitting at my side, and my eyes widened in horror. "That's Mr. Oakman, my neighbor..." My voice trailed off in my terror, and Connor stared at me with his own.

"It looks like he never left the house."

"We have to tell somebody." I exclaimed as I hurried out of the building and into the parking lot, Connor not far behind.

"Wait!" He lowered his voice when he caught up to me. "Wait. Who are you going to tell?"

"Someone—anybody." I stuttered, trying to contain myself and failing. "What if he did it? What if—all this time—the man who took Heather was living next door?" He laid his hands on my shoulders to calm me.

"We don't know that for sure—not yet. Besides, he's eighty-years-old. He might have been able to pull it off in '76, but not now. It has to be somebody else, this time." He scrambled for words—an explanation—anything to keep me from spiraling. I sighed.

"Who else could it be?" I thought the idea of not knowing what happened to Heather was so much worse; but now, I knew I was wrong.

"We'll figure it out." He brought his hands back to his sides and glanced at the watch on his wrist. "Come on. We're gonna be late." He started sprinting towards the sidewalk, only stopping when he realized that I wasn't following him.

"Late for what?" He smiled at my question.

"For breakfast. You know how fast Mrs. Harrison's chocolate croissants go." With that, Connor darted across the empty street; and I shook my head with a smile before I joined him.

The smell of freshly baked apple pie filled my nostrils as I slid into my seat at the booth in the corner furthest from the door, a jumble of words from the other patrons' conversations occasionally reaching our table. They were fraught with plans for the rest of the day: some would be going to the bowling alley or spending most of the afternoon at the closest mall. I watched as customers went in and out of the restaurant, listened quietly to all that surrounded me. There, at the table near the glass case of doughnuts and bagels and other assorted pastries, sat a mother and her child hoisted up in a booster seat. I grinned to myself when I witnessed her cut a small piece of her pancake with the side of her fork and feed it to him.

That would be me, someday; but I would be sitting in my dining room, and my husband would be making pancakes with the raisins he mistook for chocolate chips. This was something I'd imagine often, late at night when I couldn't sleep. But it was always the same in that...I could never see his face.

"Hey guys. What can I get you?" The familiar voice shattered my thoughts, pulling me out of the maze of my imagination. I looked up at her face; and for a second, I swore that it was Heather standing before us. But it was fourteen-year-old Natalie Harrison that smiled back at me.

A year without her sister had changed her—so much, the pigtails she had worn in January disappeared into a single ponytail; and a touch of makeup had found its way onto her freckled face.

"Hi—um…" I stuttered, but Connor kept me from finishing.

"I got it." He reassured me and turned to Natalie. "Could we have a stuffed French toast with bananas, a ham and cheese croissant, two glasses of milk, and a bowl of olives, please?"

"Sure." She replied as he handed her the two menus that had been sitting on our table. "I'll be back soon." I waited until she stepped away from us to speak.

"We have to find out what happened to the Bannekers." I said, and he hastily glanced around the room to see if anyone was listening.

"They probably moved." He whispered in response.

"And left the house to Mr. Oakman?" I asked him, doubtful. "He could have the whole family buried in his basement."

"You don't really believe that, do you?" I placed my hand on my forehead in frustration and leaned back in my seat.

"No. But there has to be something we're missing." I sighed to myself.

"What about the other girl—April Lawson?" For a moment, I shut my eyes, desperate to know why the name of a girl who disappeared sixty years ago sounded so familiar.

"Lawson?" I opened them at the sound of her voice. "You said something about Lawson?" Natalie inquired as she set our two glasses of milk onto the table. Connor and I locked eyes before I answered.

"Yeah. We were just wondering if there was anyone in town with that last name." I told her; and she smiled, chuckling a little at my question.

"Well, yeah. That's my grandma's maiden name. That whole side of the family's lived here forever." She stole a look over her shoulder, grinning when she returned her attention to the silence of the table. "I'll be back with your food in a few." I took in a deep breath as I watched her leave, mortified.

"Connor —" I didn't need to finish.

"Yeah. I know." I guess it was time for that visit.

Connor paused at the door, looking back at me for an answer.

"Are you ready?" I nodded, swallowing hard. "Okay." He rapped his knuckles twice against the whitewashed wood; and then, we could only wait, my own legs swaying in apprehension. I heard the floor creak beneath the feet of who I could only guess would be Heather's father; but when the door was unlocked and pulled open, it was her grandmother standing in the doorway.

"Hello." She spoke with such an airy voice, her words barely reached my ears. "Melissa and Connor, it's been so long. Please, come in." She moved backwards to let us step inside, and I was instantly overwhelmed with the ghosts Heather left behind. Nothing of hers had been touched since she disappeared, in such a way that the Harrisons' residence had become a vault of memories; and I remembered why I hadn't visited more often.

There she was: sitting on the couch as I taught her how to braid her hair, coming in from the kitchen with a bowl of olives for Connor, questioning his obsession for the hundredth time, or leaping down the stairs to show us the dress she had just bought for her first date with Matthew.

I stared down at the glass coffee table in the center of the room when I found my seat next to Connor on the couch, and the glint of a silver ring caught my eye.

"You can take it," I looked up at the old woman as she sank into the armchair across from us, "if you want it. Poor Hannah just keeps everything—won't let anyone move them out of place. Almost a year has passed. I think it's time this house stops being a graveyard." I reached out to take the ring from the reflective surface and held it tightly in my fingers.

"Thank you." I whispered, and I cleared my throat when my voice suddenly cracked.

"We actually wanted to speak to you," Connor paused, "about April Lawson?" I watched as the little girl emerged in her eyes at the sound of her older sister's name.

"April." She sighed and folded her hands in her lap with a doleful smile. "She loved the water—always found an excuse to go to that lake. And I was always behind her, shadowing her like the little sister that I was." Something about her shifted, and the child in her eyes seemed to die as she recalled the rest. "But that night was different." She gazed at the floor as she spoke, getting lost in that horrible memory. "She wanted to go late at night, while our parents were asleep. We rode our bicycles to the water's edge. April went first—called me a worry wart for not jumping in right away. She said that night was supposed to be special, and she was right. It was just us two; and the sky was so bright, like it wasn't midnight at all." She glanced up at the ceiling as if she saw the sky as it was that fateful night, her eyes darting about at the stars that didn't exist. "And then," she stared at us finally; and I could see the pain that only Natalie would understand, "she was gone."

"The newspaper article said the sky was different." I leaned forward as I asked. "What did they mean?" She faltered for a moment before gazing at me blankly. "Was it a full moon?" Her eyes widened—not in alarm, but in something so much deeper. And I realized that it was terror, as if she were sitting across from a corpse and not a person.

"It was." She admitted, and her mousy tone returned. "But it was so much more than that."

"How's that?" Connor wanted to know.

"It was a blue moon." She simply said; and I could only stare back at her, unsure of what that meant.

"What's a blue moon?"

"It's the second full moon in a month." It was Connor that answered my question, and the idea suddenly sent a chill running down my spine.

"When Heather disappeared, I knew that it was happening again. But no one believed me then, so why should they believe me now?" She frowned; and I remembered feeling the same in Mr. Thompson's class, surrounded by stares of pity and cautiousness.

"We believe you." Abigail looked at me with sadness as I twiddled my thumbs. "I—I know what it's like."

"Then, there's something you should know." From the way she looked at us, with a terror I couldn't comprehend, I already knew.

"There's going to be another blue moon, isn't there?" I asked her, my voice trembling in my throat. And the nod of her head confirmed my fears. "When?" She sighed once again; but this time, it was one of unbridled dismay.

"New Year's Eve." I turned to Connor, but his horror seemed to be far greater than mine.

New Year's Eve.

Two days after my sixteenth birthday.

Chapter Five

Photographs on the Wall

The last bell of the school day rang shrilly in my ears, rattling my thoughts until they floated in bits and pieces in my head. I looked up from the notebook in my hands as I sat in the grass underneath the net of the soccer goal, and a surge of students came rushing out of every door of the buildings standing in the distance. They scattered as they found their own path across the soccer field; and I watched as one of them sprinted towards me, only grinning when I recognized the head of blonde hair that came into view.

"Hey." He greeted me breathlessly. "I thought I'd find you here." Connor let the backpack he carried over his shoulder slump to the ground as he knelt down to join me. "You missed sixth period. That's not like you." I closed my notebook and set it down, and he glanced at it in curiosity. "What were you writing?"

"My project for my writing class — Mr. Thompson says 'write what you know,' but," I sighed, "I can't."

"Why not?" He asked me.

"My writing scares people." I said, and he playfully set his hand on my shoulder.

"But you do it so well." He joked, only pausing in his laughter when he saw the look of discouragement on my face. "All right — what do you have so far?"

"It's about a little girl whose family dies while she's at a sleepover with her friends — "

"Sheesh." Connor interjected.

"You asked…" I replied with a hint of a smile on the corner of my lips.

"Well, what happens next?" He asked me with genuine interest, and I couldn't help but let that smile linger much more freely.

"She returns home to find their ghosts waiting for her like they never died; but only a short time after she resumes living there with her grandparents, she realizes that her family is repeatedly reliving their last day." It seemed so much darker when I said it out loud.

"That's really sad." He remarked, frowning.

"It is." I said as I rose to my feet, and toting my backpack over my shoulder, turned to wait for Connor as he did the same.

"But I don't see anything wrong with it. It's a good story. How does it end?" He inquired, falling prey to his curiosity.

There was almost nothing he didn't want to learn about. I grinned a little when I remembered how his questions about horses became too difficult for my father to answer.

"I don't know yet..." My voice trailed off as I found myself lost in thought, still clinging to the fibers of a story yet to be finished. Hastily, I pulled my cell phone from my pocket and flipped it open. "It's three o'clock. My mom's probably here, by now."

"Oh—okay." He stuttered as we stepped across the soccer field. "Are you coming to my game tonight?"

"Can't." I sighed to myself as I spoke.

"I'm working at the ranch again."

"Really?" I didn't have to look at him to recognize the disappointment in his voice. "On a game night?"

"You're the one who made me late. This way, she punishes the both of us." I told him once we reached the paved walkways of the school. It had only been a few minutes since the final bell; but in that time, the place had become as hollow as a drum. A couple freshmen hurried past us in the opposite direction, shrinking bashfully at the sixteen-year-old walking by my side. I smiled quietly to myself, but Connor—he didn't notice.

"It was one time," he argued, "and you weren't even that late."

"It's not so much as my being late, I think." It was hard to put into words, and I stared at the concrete path as I spoke them. "It was a full moon, and you know how parents get around that time." Connor nodded in understanding as he kicked a crumpled piece of paper up from the ground.

"I guess." He looked up at me, pausing as a thought suddenly occurred to him. "Have you noticed—" I glanced at him when he stopped.

"What?"

"I don't know—your mom..." He ran his fingers through his hair as he scrambled to explain. "She's been...kinda weird, lately." I shrugged my shoulders at the idea.

"She's just worried about me." I said, and the familiar whir of running engines and chattering students finally found its way into my ears. "With losing Heather and all those girls going missing—" I turned to face him when we stopped at the edge of the sidewalk, where it ended and the parking lot began. "Yours doesn't have anything to worry about."

"Nothing's going to happen to you." He reassured me, but I couldn't help but wonder if that were true.

"Are you sure?" I chuckled a little, if only to stop the heart that relentlessly fluttered in my chest.

"I won't let it." With a wink, he reached out to punch my shoulder; and he stole a quick look over his shoulder. "I've got to go—practice for the game and all." He readjusted his backpack over his back and sprinted a few steps away, halting when I called out to him.

"Make a basket for me!"

"I...can't guarantee that!" He started to run backwards as he responded, and I laughed when he collided with a group of students that proceeded to jostle past him.

"Melissa, hon, are you ready to go?" I looked down at my mother's blue car when I heard her voice.

"Yeah." I pulled open the door and set my backpack on the floor before sliding inside.

"How was your day?" She asked.

"Fine." There it was: the ultimate teenage answer. I never thought I'd reach that point; but then, everything was changing. I just didn't know how much.

"How is everyone doing so far?" I called out to the half dozen horses ahead of me and smiled when Mason shouted his answer.

"We're doing just fine, Miss Moonwater." He reassured me, turning his head towards the little boy riding a pony behind him. "Isn't that right, Liam?"

"Yep!" He nodded enthusiastically.

"That's my man." Mason said, grinning as he tipped his hat Liam's way. We continued down the dirt path, the ground too cold to be easily disturbed by the hooves that passed over it; and a grove of trees came into view. They were bare now, just the bones of what were once covered in leaves as green as Connor's car.

Connor. I sighed. The game would be starting soon, and I was miles away.

"Hey, Moongirl." I pulled on the reins to slow Artemis down and stole a glance over my shoulder.

I'd only heard that voice once before, but it wasn't one that I had forgotten.

"I thought I'd come through the front door this time." Caleb explained with a smile.

"Hey, Mason, I've got to stay back for a while." I called to him before jumping down from the white horse's back.

"Sure thing!" He replied, almost too far away for me to determine what he had said.

"What are you doing here?" I asked him, feigning annoyance.

"I thought I'd take some horseback riding lessons." I made a face at his words. "What? Not convinced?" He dismounted his own horse to step towards me. I shook my head.

"You seemed to be doing just fine. Now if you'll excuse me, I have to get back to work." I remarked and started to move in the other direction.

"I think I've got you figured out." He said, and I slowed in my steps.

"You think so?" I scoffed, but there was a curiosity I couldn't suppress.

"I do." He answered me. "The girl who

disappeared — she was your friend, wasn't she?" I sighed heavily as I ran my fingers through Artemis' mane.

"Which one?"

"Heather." I turned to face him sharply when I heard him speak her name; and for a moment, I wished I'd shot him in the barn that night.

"That's none of your business." I snapped, angry; but he took a step closer.

"The woman at the newspaper —" I wouldn't let him finish.

"That was you?" I walked towards him, still unsure of what I was going to do.

"I heard about what was going on. I just didn't know it was that close to home." He glanced down at his shoes as he spoke. "Listen, I understand."

"No, you don't." I stormed in the opposite direction; but something grasped my hand, holding me back.

It was strange, but all too familiar — like the drops of water that had clung to my skin when I had stood at the edge of the abandoned bridge. I looked down, only to see that Caleb had curled his fingers around mine.

"Let go of me." I tore away from him and climbed onto my horse's back, gripping her reins once I regained my balance.

"I was late." He buried his hands in his pockets as he stared at the frozen ground. "We were," he sighed, "going to go on a walk. It was something we did...every now and then. But when I got to the house — when I got to the house, the lights were off. And it didn't make any sense, you know? No one else was home but her, so I thought maybe — maybe she just forgot and went out do something else. But...then I saw the blood, so I followed it. And I found her, but her head—" His voice cracked, and I watched him hastily wipe the tears away from his eyes.

He didn't have to say anymore.

"We grew up together." He looked up at me when I began. "She went out to go swimming one night, and she never came back."

"They never found her?" He asked.

"No." I swallowed and suddenly found my feet touching the ground.

"I think it helps," he paused, "making sure they're remembered." I almost smiled.

"It does."

"You're kidding. She did *not* do that every time."

"I'm serious. She'd do it every time we went to her mother's restaurant. It was ridiculous." I told him as we walked past the corral, leading the last of the horses out of the cold and into the shelter of the barn.

"And the waiters would just go along with it?" He asked, still doubtful that it was true; and I glanced over my shoulder at him as I answered.

"Her whole family owned the place. If she said it was Connor's birthday, it was Connor's birthday."

"Hmm…" He looked down at the floor as he chuckled to himself. "It sounds like she was a good friend."

"The best." I smiled, thinking of all the times Connor's face had flushed a bright red when he saw the entire staff rounding the corner with sparklers.

"Thanks for staying after hours, son." My father spoke as he leaned against the stall door, obscuring most of Poseidon's nameplate with his back.

"It's a pleasure, Mr. Moonwater." Caleb said and reached out to shake his hand; but when their palms touched, my father held him there, staring at him in curiosity.

"What's your name?" He wanted to know.

"Caleb—Caleb Ahoka." He answered; and my father let him go, satisfied.

"Ahoka…strong name. Where are you from, Caleb?" My father asked him as he took Athena's reins from my hands and led her into her stall.

"I was born in Georgia," he told him,

burying his free hand in his pocket, "but my family moved here when I was really little."

"Well, it's nice to have you here." My father patted him on the back once he locked Athena's door.

"It's nice to be here." He paused. "What's that?" I stared at him, oblivious.

"What's what?" And then I heard it.

I've got friends in low places...

But it wasn't the incomparable Garth Brooks singing the words.

"Oh." I reached into my pocket with my right hand and pulled out my phone, flipping it open to look at the screen. The sound of Connor's voice suddenly came to an end, and his name appeared over the message he had sent me.

S,s:O.

What did that mean?

"Hey, I've gotta go." I murmured, so low I wasn't sure if anyone had heard me. "Dad," I turned to face him; and he looked to me expectantly, "could we have Mason and Henry close up for the night? I think Connor's in trouble."

"'Course, kiddo. I'll just let Mason know." He nodded and hurried towards the door, leaving the two of us in the quietness of the night.

"I guess that's my cue." Caleb started, beginning to walk in the same direction; and I bit my lip for a moment as I watched him leave.

"Wait. Caleb?" He stopped just short of the doorway.

"Yeah, Moongirl?" There was that smile again.

"We have free riding lessons for kids under seven—you know, if you want to bring your brothers again." *Why did I say that?*

But he chuckled and nodded his head.

"I'll keep that in mind." And then he was gone.

It was quiet. No bright lights—just darkness and silence in the dimly lit room. In the minutes that I had spent on my way home, every nightmare had found its way into my imagination; and still, as I gazed at him from the hallway, the first replayed in my mind.

Just like that Monday, I'd wake up; and my world would be in pieces.

I stood in the doorway, as still as everything else around me; and I looked up at the woman by my side.

"I tried to keep him from texting, but he said it was an emergency." She crossed her arms as she spoke.

"Thank you, Mrs. Reilly."

"Of course." She grinned and set her hand on my shoulder before turning to leave.

"Connor?" I whispered his name as I rushed to his bedside, bending down to his level. "What happened?" His chest expanded with the air that stole into his lungs as he placed his hand on his forehead, and I saw the bandage covering his temple.

"Took a header in the beginning of the second half—don't really remember what happened next." He breathed; and I let out a sigh of my own, shrugging.

"Well…you won."

If that was any consolation…

"We did?" His eyes lit up as he lifted his head from his pillow. "Then it was totally worth it." He laid his head back on his pillow and grinned to himself.

"They said you have a concussion…" I frowned.

"I'm…fine." He insisted, but he grimaced as he attempted to sit up in his bed. "The room's just spinning, is all." I rose with him, and he gestured for me to join his side.

"You sure?" He nodded. "Okay." I said, sitting beside him; and for a moment, we sat together in silence. I leaned my head on his shoulder as I stared at the opposite wall, and I smiled at the pictures that lined it.

All of them—they told a story that stretched over the years: one of a little boy who moved from a great big city to a very small one and met a girl with a funny name and another who insisted everyday was his birthday. But sitting with him, I wondered—would the pictures return to just that little boy, all grown up now, all by himself?

I stole a glance at him, only to find that his eyes were closed; and gently, I took his hand in mine.

"Thanks for coming." He murmured softly.

"Never left."

Chapter Six

Life and Death, Death and Life

"Somebody! Somebody help me!"

I sat up in the darkness of my bedroom, struggling to catch my breath. In my heart, I knew the nightmare was over; but Heather's screams still filled my ears. The alarm clock on my bedside table suddenly began to blare, and I sighed as I hastily pushed the OFF button. I fell back onto the mattress and lay there in the silence, staring up at the ceiling covered in stars.

Just two more days like this. Two more days, and school would be out for the next two weeks.

I forced myself to stand and groggily shuffled to my door, pushing it open as I stepped into the hallway. It was cold and empty, as it always was when I first woke up. Everyone was still asleep—everyone but me. Blindly, I found the bathroom at the end of the hall and turned on the light; and instantly, I had to blink away the spots that riddled my vision. I shed my Oklahoma City Thunder T-shirt and left it on the floor, and goosebumps erupted all over my skin.

Winter was almost here; but in some ways, it seemed like it already was.

I hesitated as I turned the knob in the shower, knowing that it would be freezing, and let the water fall from the showerhead and into my hand. I waited quietly as it warmed and pulled back the curtain to climb inside. The goosebumps melted away as the water rolled down my neck and onto my back; and for a moment, I closed my eyes, just to feel it falling all around me.

But then, there was another scream — one that didn't sound like Heather at all; and I knew that it was I who was drowning. I cried out, horrified as I began to sink into the murky water; but just as every time before, nobody was coming. I flailed my arms, lungs burning when I gasped for air and found none; and as I fought for myself, I knew that I was going to lose.

"Melissa?" My mother's distant voice pulled me out of the darkness; and I found myself on my knees, clutching the knob with fingers white with terror.

"Yeah?" I answered hoarsely.

"I heard you scream. Did you fall? Are you okay?" She asked from the hallway.

"Yeah, Mom. I'm all right." I knew she

wouldn't believe me. I didn't believe myself.

"Okay, sweetheart." She paused. "I'll be downstairs making breakfast."

But it didn't stop her from pretending that she did.

The sound of creaking floorboards faded away as she left the hallway, and I was alone again. It was only after she was gone that I realized that the water had stopped, and I unclenched my hands from the knob and swept the hair from my eyes.

"What?" I blinked, unsure of what I was seeing. I hadn't moved it at all. I turned it back and forth, wondering if somehow the water had frozen in the pipes; but I knew it wasn't likely. Rising to my feet, I sighed; and suddenly, all at once, a million droplets of water plummeted to my feet. I turned my head sharply in alarm, looking for an explanation.

But there was none.

"Hey, there." My mother called to me from the kitchen. I finished the last few steps of the staircase and stopped in the living room.

"Where's Dad?" I asked her, a little confused.

"He went to check on the horses early."

That's strange.

He didn't do that very often.

"Why?" I wanted to know, hurrying into the kitchen for my answer. She stole a quick glance at me before returning her attention to the stove. Bacon sizzled in the pan before her, and the waffle iron's presence on the counter made me smile. Those were reserved for a special occasion. "It's not…" My voice trailed away; and when she grinned in return, I sprinted to the front door. Excitedly, I pulled it open; and immediately, a ball of white spiraled towards me, hitting me square in the chest. It disintegrated on impact; and as I gathered my senses, Connor's and Matthew's laughs echoed in my ears. "How long were you two standing there?" I brushed the snow from my shirt as I spoke.

"About an hour." He shrugged and hurled another at my shoulder. "It gave us time to make a couple dozen."

"I'm gonna kill you!" I hurried down the steps and into the snow and grabbed a fistful up from the ground.

"Wait! Wait!" He held up his hands in surrender. "I have a concussion, remember?" He exclaimed, and I slowed on my way to greet them.

"You can't hit a guy with a concussion." Matthew shrugged, grinning slightly. Connor let his arms fall to his sides, and I flashed him a clever smile.

"That was a week ago." I watched his face

twist into a look of surprise when I smashed the snow into his hair; and I turned, heading towards the door as Matthew's chuckles filled the background. "C'mon. My mom's making waffles."

"Seriously?" Connor sprinted after me and paused for Matthew at the door. "You coming, Matt?"

"Sorry." He called to him from the front lawn. "Heather's grandma saw me on the way here and asked me to join them."

"Okay." Connor nodded. "Catch you later." He waved goodbye before closing the door behind him.

"Hey, Connor." My mother acknowledged him as she started to set the table. The both of us wandered through the kitchen and into the dining room, where she was waiting with a platter of waffles. "Come sit down."

"This looks great, Mrs. Moonwater." He commented, pulling up a seat.

"You know how the first snow day is." She replied as she lowered the plate of bacon onto the table. "How's your mom?"

"Had to leave early for work, today — said it was some kind of emergency." He answered as he reached for the maple syrup, uncapping it to drown his waffles.

There was something about the quietness that unnerved me, and I stood in the living room by myself as I sought to identify it. The television—my father would have been watching it right now.

"Melissa, come and have some breakfast." My mother said, beckoning for me to join them.

"I just thought I'd turn the news on." I looked at her from over my shoulder when I responded and clicked the power button on the remote.

"And we should be expecting a few inches of snow moving into the holiday season."

The weatherman pointed to the map displayed behind him.

More snow. That'd be nice.

My mother stuck her head out of the kitchen once more to rein me in.

"Anything exciting?" I shook my head at her words and followed her. "So, since it's a snow day, do you two have anything in mind?" She asked us as I sat down at the table. Connor and I stared at each other, not entirely certain about the answer.

"Um…we might hang out, watch a movie, and play some board games?" It was more of a question than anything else; but when I looked at him, he didn't object.

"Sounds like fun." He interjected, taking another bite out of a piece of bacon.

"And we're back to Mayes County Medical Center with an update on that long-running missing persons case."

I lifted my head from my plate to listen.

"Mom, could you turn that up, please?" I requested; and she nodded, moving out of the kitchen and into the living room to pick the remote up from its place.

"Now, we're not sure whom the police found in Kellyville late last night; but we do know that she was evacuated by helicopter and brought here to be evaluated, mostly likely to be closer to her immediate family."

Connor and I locked eyes one more time; but this time, it was with absolute certainty.

Why they built a hospital right next to the cemetery is beyond me. Beyond the white walls of the medical center stood a garden of stones, silent and still in the distance. It scared me — terrified me even — almost to the point where I couldn't set foot in Pryor for any reason. The air of death was inescapable. In every corner — every street — I felt it. Waiting for me...just like it waited for everyone else.

It was only when I was older that I realized what it really was: not the result of unfortunate design, but an emblem of life — a combination of the two places our lives will always revolve around — a place we'd always come back to.

And here we were again.

Lights flashed outside the windows of Connor's Oldsmobile as we cruised past the front of the hospital and into the parking lot. A crowd had started to gather amongst the reporters that blocked the entrance; and I knew that like the two of us, the parents of the missing had come to see who had been found. I unfastened my seatbelt before he took the key out of the ignition and lunged for the handle.

"Wait." He set his hand on my shoulder. "How are we getting in?" I uncurled my fingers from around the handle and sat back in the seat, sighing deeply.

I didn't think of that.

But then, he smiled.

"What?" I stared at him, oblivious to what he might have been thinking.

"It's a hospital."

"No word yet on the identity of the victim brought here from Kellyville last night, but we are receiving news that she is in stable condition and has not sustained any life-threatening injuries."

"We've been told that the young woman brought to this hospital is indeed a resident of one of the cities from which the eleven girls have gone missing. The medical center has not yet released her name in respect for the family's privacy."

"The authorities in Kellyville have given little to no information on just where this victim was found. All we know is that she is being treated for knife wounds in this hospital behind us."

"So you know what to do?" Connor asked me as we forced our way through the thickening crowd. I nodded my head, immediately realizing that he wouldn't have heard that.

"Yeah, I've got it." I replied, not far behind. I held onto the sleeve of his coat, determined to not get swallowed up in the masses that swarmed the front of the medical center.

It was all too much—I couldn't handle it. It was almost as if Pryor in its entirety had come, just to welcome one of its daughters home.

We broke through the crowd and into the open space of the lobby; and to my relief, it was quiet. My own footsteps echoed in my ears as I approached the front desk, and I could have sworn I heard Connor's heart beating beside me.

"Hello." A woman in pink and white floral scrubs looked up at me from her computer.

"How can I help you?" She inquired with a smile.

"We were thinking about applying for an internship that we could do after school." I gestured to Connor as I spoke. "He's planning on majoring in biochemistry in college, and I'd like to learn more about your rehabilitation services."

"Oh," she grinned, "okay. We'd love to have you." She rolled her chair back to reach underneath the desk, pulling out a thin packet of

Title	MOONSHADOW (THE MOONSHADOW SERIE
Condition	Good
Description	Cover/Case has some rubbing and edgewear. Access codes, CD's, slipcovers and other accessories may not be included.
Employee	angelaa

papers. "You'll have to fill out these before you get started. It's just a formality, really. We want to know what exactly you're interested in and that your parents are onboard. In the meantime, we can give you a tour of the hospital. Pierre?" A young man with a head of curly hair stopped just short of the exit, turning at the sound of his name.

"Yes?"

"I know you were just leaving, but do you think you could show these two around a little bit before you go? They're considering applying for an internship." She asked apologetically. He shrugged, not really seeming to mind.

"Sure." He walked back through the lobby and passed us, pausing in the middle of the hallway when he noticed that we weren't following him. "You guys coming?" Sheepishly, I looked to Connor; but he was already ahead of me.

"Let's go." He said, and I hurried to catch up with him. "So, what do you do here?" Connor wondered aloud.

In his black buttoned shirt and jeans, he clearly wasn't a doctor.

"I volunteer in the children's ward." He started to explain, and I caught the hint of an accent in his voice. "With all they go through, a little laughter goes a long way." He added, stealing a glance at us from over his shoulder. "What made you want to take a look into medicine?" I opened my mouth to speak, but no explanation came out.

"My dad was a paramedic." For a minute, I stared at him, surprised at what he'd said.

It wasn't something he liked to talk about.

"What about you?" Pierre turned his attention on me, waiting for an answer. "Does it run in your family?" I shook my head as we passed by the doors leading into the emergency room.

"No." I responded. "Just horses."

"What's working in the pediatric ward like?" Connor questioned him as we strolled around the corner, and I looked up at the sign hovering over the corridor: Pediatric Intensive Care Unit.

"Well, you can see for yourself." He remarked; and a little girl came running down the hall when she caught sight of him, her dark brown hair flying behind her. "Hey, Danielle!" He exclaimed and bent down to embrace her.

"Did you forget something?" She stared at him with wide brown eyes.

"No. I just thought my friends would like to meet you." He explained to her; and she smiled broadly, revealing an incomplete set of teeth.

"Hi, Danielle." She gazed at me when I spoke her name. "I'm Melissa, and this is Connor."

"Nice to meet you." Connor said as he

reached down to shake her hand.

"Do you like my hair?" She asked us eagerly, and I nodded my head with a grin. "I just got it yesterday."

"Dani, sweetheart, it's time for lunch." I lifted my eyes from her face to see a red-headed nurse standing at the end of the hallway.

"I have to go now." She whispered, and I watched her sadly as she bounded away.

"How sick is she?" I was almost afraid to ask.

"She's not—" He paused, continuing once I furrowed my brow in confusion. "Not anymore—we've been seeing quite a few cases of the H1N1 virus here. But the doctors have been able to tackle it in time."

"What about..." I reached to touch my own hair, and he seemed to understand.

"Alopecia." He answered, unconcerned. "Nothing serious." I drew in a deep breath, and a wave of relief flooded through my veins.

Suddenly, Connor tapped my arm with the back of his hand, his eyes fixed on something to his right. I turned my head in the same direction just as a police officer shut the door of a hospital room and walked past us.

"Pierre, do you know who's staying in there?" I pointed to the third door down the corridor.

"Not a clue. I'm not allowed to go near it. But, whoever it is was brought in early this morning." He buried his hands in his pockets and shrugged. "Listen," he raised the silver watch on his wrist to his eyes, "I'm running late for something." He looked up at me. "Would you mind if I took off?"

"No. Go ahead." Connor encouraged him. "We'll find a way back."

"Great. Thanks." He waved goodbye before sprinting around the corner and out of sight. And then it was just the both of us.

"Do you think we should?" Connor didn't need to say anything to let me know what his answer was. I forced a breath of air into my lungs. "Here goes." Slowly, I stepped towards the door, stealing a glance behind me just to make sure that I wasn't alone. My hand trembled when I reached for the handle and turned it, and I had to stifle a gasp when it opened from the other side. A pair of weary eyes met me from the doorway. I recognized them — just barely, but I remembered them.

"I—I'm sorry." He stuttered. "She isn't taking any visitors, right now."

"Daddy...it's okay. Let them in." The raspy whisper sounded far away, as if only her body had escaped and left her soul behind. Hesitating, he opened the door and stepped aside.

"You need to be resting." He insisted, but she wouldn't have it.

"Please?" With that word, I knew he

couldn't deny her.

"I'll be waiting outside." He told her and slipped past us and into the hallway.

"Melissa?" She was sitting on the bed when I saw her, fading into the white blanket draped over her shoulders. The color in her hair was gone, and it shrouded her pallid face like a moldering veil. There was an eerie kind of silence as she stared at me with her broken blue eyes, and she whispered my name again through cracked lips. "Melissa?"

"Adrienne…" I rushed to the bed to wrap my arms around her, careful not to squeeze her too tightly. "I'm so glad you're okay." I let her go, desperate for answers. "What happened?" She rubbed her arms hidden underneath her blanket and gazed down at her sheets, murmuring so softly, I strained to hear her words.

"I was out on the balcony—and then, I wasn't. It was warm—like summer; but inside, it was cold and dark. I couldn't see anything…but I could hear—I could hear them screaming when he cut into their arms…and their backs…and their legs."

"How do you know what he was doing?" I think Connor already knew the answer to his question.

"He did it to me, too." Her eyes started to fill with tears as she pushed back the blanket to reveal the marks that covered her body; and I was horrified when I realized that they were letters scrawled roughly into her flesh. "He said that we weren't good enough, but he wanted us to try."

"Melissa…" Connor breathed, his eyes wide. "Look at the letters." I did what he asked and immediately saw what had frightened him.

They were broken up and jagged, but I could still make them out for what they were.

"Lyn…" I whispered to myself; and at once, a light flickered on in the maze inside my head. "Adrienne, how did you end up in Kellyville?" She closed her eyes as she ran her fingers through her hair.

"Um…I don't know. I got out, and I just kept running. I wanted to stay and help the others, but I was just so scared." The tears streamed down her cheeks, and she clutched her arms once more. "And then, I was on the island — and then, I was at the bridge."

"What island? What bridge?" Connor took a step closer.

"The one in the lake," she stared at him as if he should have already known, "and the bridge that no one uses anymore — the one they say is haunted."

"You were on Cedar Crest Island?" I needed to hear it again.

"Let's go there — all of us."

I couldn't help but shudder when I thought of Heather's words.

"How did you get from Cedar Crest Island to Crybaby Bridge? They're tens of miles away from each other." Connor had to ask. I wondered the same thing. But she shook her head, unable to answer.

"I don't know." The hospital door swung open, and Mr. Shelley sauntered in.

"I think that's enough for today." He said quietly. "Thank you for stopping by." His voice cracked as he spoke, and I knew that he was sincere.

"Of course." I nodded and tenderly laid a hand on Adrienne's shoulder before rising to my feet and moving towards the door. "Thank you for letting us stay."

"Melissa…" I whirled around when she called for me.

"Yeah?"

"I saw her—when I was there. I saw Heather."

Chapter Seven

The Path in the Snow

"So what did you tell your mom?" Connor stole a glance behind him as he trudged through the snow several feet ahead of me. He was bundled up in his black coat and leather boots, carrying two duffel bags and lugging a backpack over his shoulders.

There was no use offering to relieve him of something. He could break his ankle and keep going for a good half hour.

"Uh...that I was staying the night at Chloe's house. You?" I asked him.

"I told her I was going camping with a friend." I slowed in my steps for a moment.

"What?" He stopped at the water's edge and set the two bags down, leaning to the side to let the backpack slide off and onto the ground.

"She saw me take the tent out of the

garage, so I had to tell her something." He shrugged his shoulders as he reached for my hand to help me into the boat. I felt my feet leave the forest floor, and my eyes widened in surprise at how strong he was. "You good?"

"Yeah." I nodded my head as I straightened my clothes, and the boat rocked slightly underneath me.

"Good." He breathed. "Now, I just have to get the equipment in; and then, we can go." He grunted as he lifted one of the bags up from the ground and laid it beside me.

"Hey, Connor?" I called after him, wrapping my arms around my legs once I had sat down.

"Yeah?" He looked up just as he bent down to retrieve his backpack. I swallowed as I stared at him for a moment.

Bathed in the golden light of the setting sun, the sight of him reminded me of how long we had been friends. I didn't say anything—just stared.

"Something wrong?"

"Do you think we'll find anything?" He scratched his head at my question.

"Maybe—we have to try." I looked down at my shoes and then back to where he had been standing only to see that he wasn't there. "All right." I turned to find him setting the last bag by my side. "I think we're all set." He let out a sigh as he pushed the boat farther into the water, hurriedly swinging his legs over the side and climbing into the seat across from me when it started to drift. He pulled the cord to get the motor going, and we began to move across the water and towards the island. My hands trembled as I looked out at the rippling surface, realizing that it was the first time I'd been in it since Heather had disappeared.

Ever since that morning, the thought of water terrified me. Something that seemed so harmless — so still — destroyed a life in an instant.

"Melissa..." It wasn't until he said my name that I noticed that he was holding them to stop them from shaking. "She's not in there." He reassured me, and I nodded.

He was right. She was somewhere else — in a place that didn't make any sense.

"She said it was warm..." I muttered to myself; but when Connor set his gaze on me, I knew that he had heard it.

"What?"

"Adrienne said it was warm outside...like summer." I repeated. "How could that be true in a place like this?" He shrugged his shoulders, as confused as I was.

"I don't know." He began. "I don't understand a lot of it. The island, the bridge, the letters — I can't see the connection."

"I guess we just have to look harder..." My voice trailed away as the boat's motor suddenly stopped, falling silent yards away from the island's shore.

"Huh…that's weird." He remarked and reached for the pair of oars lying at our feet. "I guess we'll have to row the rest of the way." He handed one to me and kept the other, and I reminded myself to breathe before dipping it into the water. I brought my arms to my chest, and the boat pushed forward. I kept going, determined to find what awaited us in the trees, even when my shivering arms screamed for rest.

I couldn't stop—not until I knew.

My heart leapt into my throat when I forced the paddle into the water once more and it dug into a bank of mud. I set the oar on the floor of the boat as I watched Connor drop the other and jump out, immediately realizing that I should do the same. A chill ran through my spine when my feet touched the ground, and something told me that I should be afraid.

After all these years, I was here; and now, I wish I never came.

"What now?" I asked him breathlessly. He took a step forward and joined me in staring up at the trees that towered over us.

"Now, we look harder."

"Hey, Connor?" I called to him from within the walls of the tent, and I witnessed his silhouette steal across the side and toward the northern entrance. The partition splitting the tent in half unzipped, and he poked his head through the opening.

"Yeah?"

"I think you have my—" I stopped when he held my pillow in front of his face, and I grinned. It was still inside a pillowcase I had received when I was a little girl.

"Jack Skellington? Really?" He tossed it to me, and it brushed past the top of my head and landed in the corner.

"What?" I shrugged my shoulders and ran my fingers through my hair to fix it. "It's my favorite movie." He turned, shaking his head as he mumbled.

"Of course it is." I placed the pillow at the open end of my sleeping bag and murmured something of my own.

"Just 'cause you were a scaredy-cat didn't mean I had to be." But he heard me.

"Hey." He responded as he walked around the perimeter of the tent to fetch his backpack. "I am a man of science. Everything about that movie was weird and unnatural." I moved the flap out of the way to peer into his side of the tent and smiled.

"Well, as someone with an actual imagination, I loved it." I remarked; and although I had already turned around, I knew that he was rolling his eyes. "When did you want to start looking around?" I asked him after returning to my things.

Somehow, I'd managed to forget a flashlight and unconsciously brought a fishing knife instead.

"Connor?" I looked up from my bag when he didn't answer. "Con—" I never finished. Suddenly, he was by my side; and he gestured for me to be quiet.

"There's someone else here." He whispered. I held my breath, fearful that whoever it could have been would hear me; but as I listened in the silence, I realized that was all that it was. I reached into my bag to wrap my fingers around the knife's handle and quietly rose to my feet. "Seriously? You brought a knife?" Connor exclaimed, and I shrugged in response. Slowly, I stepped out of the tent and into the pale light of the winter sky; and I stared out into the trees that surrounded us. No movement, no sound—all proof that we were very much alone.

"Connor," I glanced over my shoulder and called to him from outside, "there's no one out here." I turned my head to gaze out at the clearing once more and found myself staring into a pair of dark brown eyes.

"Oh geez!" I breathed, placing my hand on my forehead.

"Melissa, what are you doing here?" It was Matthew's voice that echoed in my ears, but I was too preoccupied with trying to catch my breath to answer.

"Trying to have a heart attack — thanks for your help." I looked up at him in surprise. "What are you doing here?"

"Heather's grandmother told me what happened to her sister." He started to explain. "I didn't think it was a coincidence." He lowered his eyes to the blade gripped in my hand. "Wait. Were you gonna stab me?"

"Sorry. You can never be too careful." I sighed as I sheathed it in my back pocket and out of sight.

"By *stabbing* me?" He repeated, incredulous.

"Connor, it's okay. It's Matt." I called to him; and soon, he was standing beside me.

"Hey, man." He greeted him with a hint of astonishment. "What brings you here?" He asked, but I was the one who answered his question.

"He's looking for Heather, too."

"Good. We could use all the help we can get." He continued speaking even after he had disappeared inside the tent's walls. "Sunset is at 5:20 pm tonight, so I thought we'd start tomorrow and have the whole day. Since the island's perimeter is…" His words seemed to fade as he stepped farther and farther away. "Hey." This time, it was as clear as a bell; and I whirled to see him stick his head out and into the open. "Are you guys coming?" I shook my head; but still, I followed him.

I lay awake in the darkness, listening to the gusts of wind batter the sides of the tent as the night dragged on; and I shut my eyes tighter, waiting for sleep to overtake me.

It was something about the blackness—the uncertainty—that kept me from dreaming. I was afraid that it would seep into my mind and invade my nightmares, sending me back to drown in the water that awaited me just beyond the trees.

"Heather." I sat up at the sound of her name. "Heather…" I pushed the sleeping bag away and crawled to the partition, where Matthew's voice trembled on the other side. "No." Quietly, I unzipped the plastic wall only to see that he was still asleep; but the place where Connor's slumbering body should have been was vacant. "No…" I watched as he writhed in his sleep, and I wondered if I did the same. I climbed through the opening and knelt down by his side, suddenly startled when he disintegrated the silence with a scream. "No!" He sat up violently; and in the moonlight that glowed across the ceiling, I could see the sweat that beaded on his forehead. He turned his head frantically, unaware of my presence.

"Matt." I spoke his name; and he faced

me, eyes wide like a frightened child.

"Melissa," he swallowed as he ran his fingers through his hair, "I was screaming, wasn't I?" He didn't seem surprised. I nodded. "Sorry." He peered at me, immediately apologetic. "I didn't wake you up—" I wouldn't let him finish.

"No." I looked down at my fingers. "Couldn't sleep. I guess we have the same problem."

"I'll never stop loving her." He confessed; and by the look in his eyes, I knew that he was telling the truth.

"She's lucky to have you." I stood and started to return to my side of the tent.

"Don't do what I did." I turned at his words. "Don't wait too long." I smiled a little, but it was masked with sadness.

"Wait for what?" I closed the partition and slipped on my shoes before unzipping the entrance and walking outside. The frosty air bit at my face and ears as soon as the moon's silver light touched my skin, and I hugged my arms to keep myself warm. The little snow that covered the ground crunched underneath my feet as I stepped out of the clearing and into the trees that loomed overhead. I shivered as the shadows swallowed me completely, casting me into utter darkness; but the light that fought its way through the tree branches kept me company, and I wasn't afraid. Something pushed me forward—kept me going; and I wanted to see where it would take me. I stole a glance over my shoulder, suddenly feeling as if something was watching me; but there was nothing.

Wherever Connor was, it wasn't close; and I couldn't help but wonder where he had disappeared to.

"Connor?" I called his name anyway. "Connor." I stopped, convinced that it had been of my own accord; but when I looked up, I knew that it wasn't.

There before me stood a pine tree—the tallest I'd ever seen—still heavy with leaves as green as grass. A soft breeze blew past me and carried a handful of dead leaves with it, seeming to beckon me forward; and I advanced towards it—if only in curiosity. An inexplicable warmth wrapped around me when I approached it. There was something so strange about it— strange and yet so familiar—like the raindrops that had settled on my hand. My arm stretched forward to touch the bark; but before I could run my fingers across its surface, an earsplitting scream erupted in the blackness of the night.

Connor.

I ran towards the sound, shouting his name.

"Connor! Connor!" The trees blurred around me as I ran; and as I stumbled blindly in the dark, I could have sworn that I saw something racing beside me. It was a shadow—

or an apparition—and it moved through the forest like a demon in the night. I gazed at it in horror, unaware that my foot had caught itself underneath a fallen branch hidden in the snow. I let out a cry of surprise as I fell forward, but something kept me from hitting the ground.

"Melissa! Thank God you're okay!" I looked up to see that it was Connor who was holding me in his arms. "Where's Matt?" My eyes widened, terrified.

"He's back at camp..." He grasped my hand when I spoke, and we bolted through the woods to the clearing. I paused at the mouth of the woods when we reached the campground, frozen at the mere sight of what awaited us. The tent stood in tatters, and what was left of it swayed eerily in the wind.

"Matt?" Connor's voice cracked when he called to him, but there was no answer. "Matt!" He sprinted ahead of me and dashed frantically through the tent, searching for him. When I caught up with him, the look on his face made my heart sink into my stomach. "He's not here." I stared down at the ground, disheartened; but what I saw only confirmed my fear.

"Connor..." I whispered.

"What is it—" He left the shredded walls to stand beside me, and the words never left his lips. A wide crimson path led away from the tent and into the woods; and immediately, I knew that it was blood. Without a word, he darted in the same direction.

"Connor! Connor, wait!" I shouted as I chased him, but he wouldn't listen. He stopped abruptly in his tracks and turned, trying to push me away.

"Melissa, turn around." He warned me, but a frightened whimper in the distance drove me forward.

"Help me...please." Matthew. He was lying against a tree, his blood saturating the snow in scarlet.

"Matt." I fell to my knees and placed my hand on his shoulder to reassure him. "It's going to be okay." I looked up at Connor. "Call the police." He nodded and hurried back to the tent.

"I—it happened so fast." He stuttered, his teeth chattering. "I just closed my eyes, and— and then," he groaned in agony. "I'm gonna die, aren't I?"

"No." Tears filled my eyes as I caught a glimpse of the wound that he reached for with trembling hands. A gash tore through his stomach, the flesh indistinguishable and riddled with bruises and skin hanging freely from his body; and blood gushed outward with the heightened rhythm of his heartbeat. "We're going to get some help...so you can go home." I desperately pressed my hands against the gaping lacerations in his skin and felt something soft, finally realizing to my horror that I was only thing keeping his insides from spilling out.

"Melissa…" I turned my head to face him when called me, and he shakily took my hand in his. "If you find her, t—tell her I tried." He begged, but I shook my head stubbornly.

"No. You're going home. You're going to be okay." I insisted, but my voice betrayed me; and I burst into tears. "Connor!" I yelled for him, hysterical.

"He's looking for you." I returned my eyes to Matthew's face.

"What?" I asked, breathless.

"He won't stop—he won't stop until he finds you." Those words—I'd never heard something so terrifying. "You have to…run." He struggled for air as he spoke, and blood gurgled from his mouth to leave dark red flecks scattered on his cheeks. "He won't stop…"

"I'm here. I'm here." Connor panted when he reappeared, carrying my Jack Skellington pillowcase. He bent down to hold it against Matthew's wound; but the young man screamed in horror, scrambling to get away from him.

"Matt…Matt! It's okay. It's just Connor." I tried to calm him and failed; and he stared at him, shrieking again and again. The sound made me sick, twisted my organs until I was convinced they were traveling in knots up from my abdomen and into my throat.

"Matt, it's me. Please, let me help you." Connor pleaded, but whatever it was about him that scared his friend so much didn't go away; and he backed away from him, sobbing uncontrollably.

"Get away from me! Don't let it get me! Don't let it get me!" He let out one last bloodcurdling scream, and then it was quiet. Matthew stared up at the sky with a chilling look of terror, and I watched helplessly as the light departed from his eyes.

Chapter Eight
Chocolate Chip Cookies

$\mathcal{A}$ dozen shadows passed slowly over my face, the red and blue lights seeming to flicker in slow motion as I leaned my head against the inside of the ambulance. I held the blanket tightly around me, praying fervently that it was just another nightmare; but I knew that it couldn't be.

I didn't drown; but it still felt like I was underwater, just trying to reach the surface.

I looked out at the crowd that had started to gather at the border of yellow caution tape. There were so many—just watching me—countless eyes gazing at a stranger.

That was all I was. After living among them for fifteen years, I was still a stranger.

I watched as the police wheeled the gurney into the little white van, and I couldn't stop the tears from coming again. I glanced back at the crowd and saw Dorothy, the Harrisons, and Mr. Oakman, but another two faces burst out of the sea of familiarity; and instantly, I felt worse than I already did.

"That's my daughter! I have to see her!" My mother explained to the officer that stopped my parents before they passed the caution tape. He waived them ahead, and they came darting towards me.

"Melissa, honey!" My father called out to me before they reached the ambulance; and suddenly, I was lost in an unyielding embrace.

"What happened?" My mother wanted to know, but I was afraid that I wouldn't be able to answer her. They let me go, and the words left my mouth in fragmented sobs.

"Connor and I went to the island to—to look for Heather. We didn't know that Matthew would…" I couldn't continue. I fought to keep myself together and lifted my head to see Connor standing in the middle of it all, a look of complete hopelessness on his face.

Now, I knew what it looked like when he cried.

"Connor!" He turned his head in my direction at sound of his name and at the sight of me, started to walk the other way. "Connor, wait!" I leapt out of the ambulance and sprinted to him, leaving the safety of my parents' arms behind.

"Please, Melissa, no more." He shook his head, eyes red from weeping.

"How could we have known?" I tried to reason with him, but he refused to hear it.

"I just want to go home." He said and turned away, but I reached for his hand to bring him back to me.

"It's not your fault." I told him, but he held up the hands still covered in blood.

"Then what is this? *We* did this. We let it happen. We were too busy trying to be heroes. My dad tried to be a hero and look where it got him!" I took a step back, shocked at the way that he'd raised his voice at me.

Nothing I'd ever done upset him so much.

"We're not heroes. We never should have tried." He stole away from me, but I called his name one last time.

"Connor, don't leave." I begged him, tears streaming down my cheeks; and he stood there and stared at me—as if he were looking at a stranger.

"I'm done." And he was gone. I lifted my hands to my face, disintegrating at the crimson that clung to my fingers, and stepped towards the water's edge.

"Tell her I tried."

I collapsed, crying bitterly; and I hesitated before plunging my hands in the water. It stung like a thousand needles tearing through my skin at once; but I kept them in the water, rubbing them together until they were raw. But still, Matthew's blood wouldn't go away. "Please." I wept. "Please." I looked down at the water and found myself more desperate than I'd ever been. It was avoiding me, apparently repelled by my bloodstained hands. "Please." I hung my head, forlorn. "Please, don't do this to me!" I almost shouted the last words, angry and desperate and most of all…guilty.

He died for nothing, and all I did was watch.

"That's somethin' I've never seen before." His voice. I'd never felt so relieved to hear it; but then, I thought of the water fleeing from my hands and knew that he was staring at a freak of nature. And I brought them to my lap and sobbed.

"I can't—I can't wash it off." I expected him to leave me alone, but he knelt by the water with me.

"Shhh…it's okay." He reassured me, whispering. "I won't tell anybody." I lifted my head to meet Caleb's eyes.

"How did you know?" He simply shrugged and flashed me another one of his charming smiles.

"It's a small town. News travels fast." The grin fell from his face when he saw my tears. "I'm sorry about your friend." He unwrapped the red scarf from around his neck and dipped it in the water. "Here." He gingerly took my left hand and cleaned the blood away from my fingers; and he moved on to the next, so careful, it bewildered me. He raised the scarf to my face, and I gazed at him in confusion.

"What are you doing?" I asked him.

"You wear them like scars." I let him gently wipe the tears away from my face; and he set the scarf down in the snow when he was finished.

"Thank you…" I murmured, so low I was sure he hadn't heard me.

"Anytime…" He replied as he leaned forward and placed his hand behind my head, pulling me in for a kiss. A surge of electricity ran through my body when our lips met, and I shivered in his arms.

There was something about him that felt so right, and I didn't want to let it go.

"Melissa!" We parted when my mother's voice reached our ears.

"I have to go." I whispered, and he nodded his head.

"I'll see you tomorrow." He spoke as I rose to my feet; and I glanced back at him, a million questions running through my mind.

"How will you find me?" I wondered aloud, and he shrugged again.

"I'll ask around."

I fell to my knees and draped myself over the porcelain bowl as I lost everything that I had eaten, heaving and coughing violently. Every time I closed my eyes, I saw Matthew's mangled body, just lying there in the darkness. Someone knocked on the bathroom door, and I pushed back my dark brown hair away from my reddening eyes.

"Yes?" I cleared my throat, trying to pick myself up from the floor.

"Melissa...oh, honey." My mother opened the door and sighed when she saw me, and she reached out her arms to help me up.

"I couldn't save him." I sobbed as she embraced me. "I couldn't stop it." She set her hands on my shoulders when she let go.

"Even if you never went to the island, he would have gone anyway. It was better that you were there. You made sure he didn't die alone." I wiped my tears away with the back of my hand, but they wouldn't stop falling. "Come on, let's get you upstairs." She wrapped her arms around me and led me to the bottom of the staircase; and with trembling legs, I started to climb it, my mother following close behind. The rosy light of dawn spilled in through the windows, lighting my way; and when I finally stumbled through the doorway of my bedroom,

I collapsed onto my bed and wept. "I'll be right outside—for as long as you need me." She whispered and closed the door behind her. Then I was alone. I lay on my back and stared up at the stars on my ceiling, wishing I could be taken up into the sky to join the real ones—and never come back. I turned my head to the window and watched as a wall of frost began to build against the glass; and I closed my eyes, feeling myself drift away. It wasn't long before I sank into a deep sleep, and the stars lingered in my mind.

I awoke to the smell of chocolate and brown sugar; and as I sat up in my bed, I smiled sadly to myself.

Cookies. But this time, there was no Connor to share them with; and the memories of everything that happened in the last twenty-four hours came rushing back to me.

I had lost Matthew and Connor in one night—and seen the personification of darkness. I slid off the side of the bed and slipped on my floral robe over my pajamas before slowly making my way down the steps.

"Are you a fishing kind of man?" I heard my father's voice carry up into the rafters from the living room, and I paused in the middle of the stairs to listen.

"I'd like to think so." The voice of a

young man answered nervously; and I leaned against the wall, straining to recognize it. The wooden steps creaked underneath my feet, and both my father and the visitor turned their heads my way.

"Melissa." Caleb stood at the sight of me, and I smiled weakly.

"Hi." I finished the remaining steps, and my father hurried to meet me at the bottom. "What time is it?"

"Just after two." He responded. "Some people from church dropped a few cards by this morning." I passed the coffee table to find a seat on the couch and saw that it was covered in envelopes.

"I thought the news didn't release kids' names…" I looked up from the pile of cards in confusion, and he sighed deeply.

"This town's too small for secrets." Maybe it was, but something told me that it wasn't.

"If you are just tuning in, we have been following a breaking news story of a teenaged boy being mauled to death last night while he and his friends camped on Cedar Crest Island. Little to no information has been provided detailing just what kind of animal attack it may have been, but authorities are requesting that you be on alert for coyotes in the area."

It was only when I heard those words that I realized that the television was on; and shaking his head, my father reached for the remote sitting on the kitchen counter.

"That's enough of that."

"Wait," I turned around to face him, "could you leave it on?" I asked, and he set it down silently. Caleb sat down beside me, and I grinned a little to myself. "I didn't think you were serious."

"What—me?" He made a face. "I'm always serious." I wanted to laugh, but it hurt too much.

"Cookies are ready." My mother came striding in from the kitchen, holding the crystal platter she used for them. "Here you are, honey." She bent down to leave them on the table before kissing my forehead.

"Thanks, Mom." I said as I watched her return to the other room, but my heart sank as I reached for one.

It wasn't as simple as Connor helping me with my Chemistry homework, and I didn't think it would be again.

I bit into one anyway, searching for a sliver of solace; but the warm chocolate coated my mouth and clumped in my throat. And it ached as I fought to swallow it.

"Regarding the discovery in Kellyville earlier this week, we have now learned that the kidnapping victim, now identified as sixteen-year-old Adrienne Shelley, was found near the site of what used to be Crybaby Bridge, a place additionally infamous for the

prank of a young couple claiming to have found its namesake in 1993 – "

I looked up when the room fell unusually silent and saw that the screen was dark, reduced to a mirror that reflected my face back to my eyes in black.

"Nathaniel," my mother spoke as she placed the remote back on the counter, "why don't you and Caleb go check on the horses?"

"Are you sure?" He almost seemed to hesitate before making his way to the door, and Caleb looked back at me in concern as he followed him.

"Yeah, we'll be fine, here. They could use the company." My mother shrugged, nonchalant; but something about the way she spoke didn't seem right.

"Okay. But if you need anything, you know where to find us." My father's eyes flew to me for a moment, and then he and Caleb disappeared into the grayness waiting outside. For minutes, it was quiet; and I sat in apprehension of what would break the silence.

My mother—was that who she was? I wasn't sure if I knew anything anymore. But she *had* known about the bridge, and that was enough to terrify me.

She stepped around the couch to sit next to me and folded her hands in her lap, keeping her eyes on her fingers.

"It found you, didn't it?" The words

stopped my heart in my chest.

"How did you—" I whispered the beginning of a question, but it was one I wouldn't have a chance to finish.

"I knew it'd be best if you heard it from me." She started. "I'd just hoped it wouldn't have had to happen this way." Goosebumps prickled over my skin, and I ran the palms of my hands over my arms in an attempt to chase them away.

"Happen what way?"

"I was never very adventurous. I—I just went along with your father. He loved that sort of thing. It was raining that night, and I remember thinking of how strange it was that it wasn't snowing. I'd heard all the stories, but I didn't," she paused to clear her throat, raking her fingers unsteadily through her hair, "I didn't think that they were true." I stared at her, unsure of what she was saying. "We were only there for a couple minutes before I saw her. She was surrounded in this bright blue light, almost rippling like she was made of water. She was crying, saying something about her baby. At first, I thought that she was looking for it—all of the legends describe the ghost of a woman searching for her child—but she wasn't." My mother took in a deep breath and finally set her eyes on me. "She wanted me to take her." I blinked.

"Her..." The revelation came slowly, in

part by my reluctance to accept what she was telling me. Of a story told a thousand times and never considered to be truly real. Of what she'd seen that night that had convinced her otherwise.

And what that meant for me.

"She asked me to keep her safe—begged me to maintain her ignorance of magic and the supernatural—even the Cherokee folk tales my grandfather would share with me when I was a child." The hint of a smile found its way into the corners of her lips, and I recognized it as the one she wore in the late afternoons at Moonwater Ranch—the only place she could speak his words into life. "Your father called for me; but when I turned back around, she was gone. And I was left with this beautiful baby girl." Tears gathered in her eyes as she gazed at me; and all of a sudden, I couldn't breathe.

"What day did you find her?" I didn't have to ask to know the answer. She wiped the tears away with her thumbs, two glistening trails on her cheeks the sole evidence that they existed.

"December 29th, 1993."

"You're saying I'm the baby—of Crybaby Bridge." Even the words that left my lips seemed foreign—syllables of a language I could speak but couldn't dream of understanding.

But if they were true—if my mother wasn't mistaken, it would change everything.

"How is that even remotely possible?"

Chocolate Chip Cookies

"You went to see it—the night your classmate Adrienne went missing." She leaned forward. "Did you notice anything unsettling or—or strange?" She sighed again when I shook my head. But something in me gave me pause. And I remembered the word scrawled into the rusted metal and the storm that followed on the heels of my voice. "What is it?"

"I…" I couldn't tell her. "I saw something…on the island. I was alone." In the quiet between my words, I found myself there again. Staring up at the tree that pulled me towards it with whispers, peering into the shadows and seeing the perversion of a human face, holding Matthew's bloodied hands as snowflakes collected on my eyelashes. "But I think Matthew saw it too." She drew back at first, unable to conceal the horror underneath her reserved expression. "He said 'he' was looking for me. Do you know who that is?"

"She never told me. She just asked to keep her—keep you—away from the darkness." She frowned. "But it looks like I couldn't even do that right."

"Mom…" She lifted her eyes from her hands when I grasped them tightly. "Do you remember what you told me when I was younger?" She didn't reply—but allowed herself to smile sadly in the moment. "I'm a Moonwater. And the moon only ever shines in the darkness."

Chapter Nine

Daffodils

Tck. Tck. Tck.

My eyes fluttered open at the sound, and I buried my face in my pillow to go back to sleep.

Tck. Tck. Tck.

I sat up, yawning, and moved my hair out of my face before glancing at the clock.

7:37 am.

The sun had barely found its way into the sky, burning brightly over the horizon; and all I wanted to do was close my eyes. But whatever it was that waited outside my window wouldn't let me.

Tck...tck.

I sighed, wishing I could have stayed where I was; but my curiosity bested me, and I couldn't help but wonder what was tapping

Daffodils

against the glass. Reluctantly, I rose to my feet and stepped towards the window, rubbing my eyes before setting them on the sky. Outside, the rose and lavender clouds vanished in the light of the morning sun; and a few beams of citrine light fell on the rooftops that filled the horizon.

Tck!

I jumped back, blinking as something suddenly hit the windowpane; and I hastily stepped forward once again to gaze down at the street below. And then I smiled.

"What are you doing?" I whispered, leaning out to stare at him in disbelief.

"Throwin' wood chips at your window." He shrugged as he swung his arm to hurl another; and I glanced up as it sailed over my head, closing my fingers around it before it could fly any farther. "Nice catch."

"What are you *really* doing here?" I asked him and let the little piece of wood tumble from my hand and settle at his feet.

"Why don't you come down here and figure it out?" He taunted me, but the smile fell from my face when I remembered what day it was.

"I can't." I frowned, slowly closing the window. "I have to go to a funeral today."

"Wait! Wait." He called out to me; and regretfully, I paused to listen. "I know." It was quiet for a moment as he lowered his eyes. I struggled to retain a single breath as my eyes

146

burned, but there were no tears left for me to cry. And then he raised them, breaking the silence. "But can I show you somethin'?"

"Sure." I sighed and shut the window, slipping on my robe before hurrying downstairs. I stopped in front of the door and ran my fingers over my hair to fix it. Turning the handle, I pulled it open and found Caleb standing on the other side.

"I remembered seein' it that night, but I didn't realize what it was 'til now." He rushed inside, shivering as he held his arms.

"Seeing what?" I asked him as I closed the door. He turned to face me as he pushed his hood from his head, suddenly serious.

"Where I found you, there were trees." He breathed. "The first time I saw it, I thought it was it was just one; but it was all of them." I stole a step back, afraid of what he saying.

"I don't follow." I shook my head, but he continued.

"Letters—three letters every time. And then what they were sayin' about the girl that was found on the news…" And then, I did. The word that had been carved into Adrienne's skin again and again had become Cedar Crest's latest mystery, one that I wasn't sure if I wanted to be solved. "It's a name."

"A name?" I had to repeat it to make sure I had heard him correctly. He nodded in response and reached into his pocket to retrieve a folded up piece of paper.

"It's old — not a lot of people use it now, but I wanted to tell you right away." I hesitated as he handed it to me, terrified of what I would find; but still, I opened it — and immediately understood. "It means 'water'."

Everything came rushing at me all at once: the bridge, the rain, April Lawson, Heather, Matthew...

My knees buckled underneath me, and I sank into my father's chair.

"It's me..." I looked up at Caleb in horror, and he hurried to join me. "What if it's been me this whole time, and he just doesn't know what I look like?" He stared at me, and I could see the confusion on his face. "Before Matthew died, he told me someone was looking for me — that 'he' wouldn't stop until he found me. The first time I saw that name, it was scratched into Crybaby Bridge."

I remembered standing there, looking over the edge and imagining the woman and her baby trapped in the car as it sank into the river — never realizing that I had known them both — known the story far more than I thought.

"What do you know — about that place?" I had to hear it from him. Maybe if he said it, then it would be easier.

"A woman was escapin' from her husband one night when she drove her car over the bridge, but it went over the edge..." He paused. "Her baby was never found."

"My mother told me a woman surrounded in a blue light gave her a baby sixteen years ago." I told him, and his eyes widened in surprise. "I think he wants her back."

"But it's a ghost story." He insisted.

"I know." I answered solemnly, knowing exactly what I was saying. I gazed down at the floor, my own eyes filling with tears as it occurred to me. "Every night, I drown…" I raised my head to glance at him. "…in my dreams. What if they're memories?"

"If you're a ghost," he lifted his hand to caress my cheek, "how could I do this?" I blushed as he brought his hand back to his side.

"I don't think it's that simple." I whispered, and he chuckled to himself.

"When is it ever?"

"I could be a shade or—or undead—" He stopped me before I could finish, silencing me with a kiss.

"Whatever you are, whatever happened that night—it made you special. It gave you—"

"Please don't say 'superpowers'." I interrupted him, shaking my head.

"Why not?" He replied, taking hold of my hands. "Dead or alive, you can stop what's going on."

"I'm fifteen…How am I supposed to do anything?" I couldn't help but wonder aloud.

Daffodils

"You can. I know you can." He said; and for a moment, I believed him. And then, I didn't.

"I don't think it's that simple." I responded once again; but this time, he lowered his eyes and exhaled in what sounded like the troubled sigh of someone who understood.

"It never is."

I stared up at the steeple as the bells rang, loud and clear in my ears; and one by one, the peals kept my heart from beating. I pushed the car door open and sighed, stepping out into the winter air. I looked out at the other black spots that riddled the great expanse of white that lay before me and wondered what we looked like from above.

I guess I wouldn't know until the picture standing at the altar was mine.

"Melissa, honey, are you coming?" My mother's voice pulled me out of my thoughts, and I realized that I hadn't moved.

"Yeah." My voice cracked as I spoke, and I cleared my throat before catching up to her. The church doors swallowed us as we walked inside, and I was welcomed with a warmth I hadn't felt for days. There were so many people—it seemed unreal as I stepped down the aisle in silence, closer to the casket that looked all too familiar. Daffodils and lilacs. The definitions hidden in the petals all seemed so meaningless now. Innocence and happiness— they died the minute the three of us set foot on that island.

We'd lost more than we could have ever gained, and I'd left Cedar Crest Island more alone than I had ever been.

"Do you think — do you think she made it?"

I turned to face the doorway, suddenly standing in an empty sanctuary; and in the last pew, I saw him sitting there…beside a girl that I didn't know anymore.

"She had to." I insisted, my voice falling away into a whisper. "She had to."

"How can you be sure?" His own voice trembled as he spoke, and I knew that he was fighting tears that came anyway. He gazed down at the daffodil he still held in his hands, and I saw his eyes gloss over as he tried to catch his breath.

"She's my best friend…" I started. "If I went missing, she wouldn't give up on me. I won't give up on her."

"Then I won't." He resolved; and when he lifted his eyes to look at me, I saw something different in them — something brighter.

I watched as the apparitions were replaced by the faces that had haunted me since the night the light in Matthew's eyes had disappeared, and it was too much. Leaving my mother's side, I sauntered back up the aisle and to the open doors, trying my best not to bump into anyone in the process. And as what little sunlight began to touch my face, I found myself staring into a pair of sad blue eyes.

"Connor…" I breathed, a little surprised to see him.

It'd been three days, but I could still see the tears streaming down his face—and hear his voice as he shouted at me in the darkness.

He lowered his eyes and silently walked past me, and I could feel my heart shattering in my chest. For a moment, I stood there, wordless as others shuffled into the church and out of the cold.

A year had changed so much.

I bit my lip as I hurried through the sea of black and into the white world beyond the doors, forcing back the tears I so desperately wanted to cry; and I leaned against the wall as I struggled to breathe.

"You were there, weren't you?" I turned my head towards the one who had asked the question, blinking.

I didn't recognize him.

"Yeah." I nodded, whispering. He buried his hands in his pockets as he took a step towards me, his breath turning to puffs of mist as he spoke again.

"How'd you do it?" I looked at him sharply, twisting my face in confusion.

Only Caleb knew, only he had seen—or at least, that's what I'd thought.

"I don't know what you're talking about." I told him, hoping he would leave me alone and join the others; but he stayed there, narrowing his brown eyes as he studied my face. I pulled myself up from the wall and stared at him in return, immediately remembering where I had seen him.

The night of Adrienne's party — the night she'd disappeared — he'd been there, too.

"It's something, isn't it? That you keep finding yourself in these situations." And then I understood. I knew exactly what he was saying.

"I'm sorry — who are you?" I squinted at him, the anger he had incited audible in my voice. I crossed my arms when he inspected me with his eyes one last time, squirming underneath my skin as if I had been violated.

"I'd rather not say. You might be going to my funeral next." He remarked and stepped backward before turning to leave, but Connor intercepted him. "You gonna let me pass?" Tension thickened the air as they merely stared at each other; and when Connor didn't move, he brushed past him.

"How familiar are you with the human anatomy?" Connor asked him, nonchalant when he gripped his arm, forcing him back to where he had stood before. "Not much?" He continued when he didn't answer. "This, right here," he pointed to the stranger's neck, "is called the jugular vein. If I compress it just right, I could cause temporary hypoxia. Do you know what that means?" He paused, but there was no response; and I saw him lean in to whisper in his ear. "When you wake up, we'll be gone; and you're gonna have a headache." The other young man tore away from him; and with a look that I could only determine as fear, he walked away. Connor set his gaze on me and fixed the collar of his suit.

"How'd you know that was going to work?" I inquired, remaining where I was. He glanced down at his shoes and then back to my face.

"I didn't." He threw up his hands as he shrugged. "But guys like him don't really argue with science." I grinned a little at his words, and he joined me at the wall. "Are you okay?" I thought for a moment, debating in my head whether or not I should tell him; but the way he looked at me — it wouldn't be fair not to.

"There's something you should know."

Chapter Ten

"Do You Like Stories?"

"Okay." I took a deep breath and lifted the glass up from the table. "Here we go." I tipped it over, and the water spilled out of the glass and onto the wooden surface. I narrowed my eyes as I stared at the puddle in silence, but it didn't move.

"Something's supposed to be happening, right?" Connor spoke, and I placed my hand on my forehead with a sigh.

"I don't know why it's not working." I replied, frustrated.

"Well, what usually makes it happen?" He whispered the question, and I shrugged in response.

"I have no idea."

"Melissa, what are you doing?" I looked up from the table to find my mother hovering over us.

"Nothing." I answered hurriedly and reached for the towel on my lap to sop up the water.

"Well, make sure you're ready when your father comes back from the ranch." She set her hand on my shoulder. "We'll be leaving right away so we can get back before the storm." I watched as she returned to the kitchen to place another batch of gingerbread cookies into the oven.

"Storm?" Connor repeated, a hint of confusion in his light blue eyes.

"It's nothing." I told him. "The weatherman said we'll get a few more inches over Christmas." He nodded. "I'll be back." I said as I stood and stepped into the kitchen to put the towel away.

"I'm glad you two are talking again." My mother remarked, and I grinned to myself.

"Me too." I set the towel down when the doorbell rang and sprinted to answer it, but Connor was already at the door.

"Whoa!" He exclaimed once he opened it, and two little boys rushed to nearly tackle me in an embrace.

"Hi, Tyler! Hi, Trenton!" I wrapped my arms around them both and glanced up when I heard Caleb's voice.

"Careful, guys. Don't squeeze too hard." He turned to Connor and held out his hand for him to shake it. "The name's Caleb. Nice to meet you."

"Yeah, sure." Connor spoke as he did, smiling kindly as he gestured to himself. "I'm Connor." He closed the door; and Caleb stepped into the living room, unwrapping his red scarf from around his neck.

"Thanks for invitin' us, Mrs. Moonwater." He said. "We really appreciate it."

"Of course." She responded as she left the kitchen to give him a hug, cautious not to get any flour on his clothes. "Why don't you sit down? We're just waiting for Melissa's father; and then, we'll be on our way."

"Thank you, ma'am." He answered and did as she suggested, following his brothers to one of the couches.

"Do you like him?" I whispered when Connor met me by the kitchen counter.

"Yeah." He started and watched the twins marvel at the Christmas tree standing in the corner of the room. "He seems pretty cool —" He stopped and smiled when he caught sight of my face. "You do."

"What?" I furrowed my brow in an attempt to deny it, but the blood was already rushing to my face.

"Congratulations," he quipped, patting me on the back, "you've got yourself your first boyfriend." He left my side to join the boys in the living room, and I couldn't help but grin to myself at the thought of it.

"Why are you standin' over there? Come here, and sit with us." Caleb invited me, beckoning me forward; and I couldn't say no.

⁂

I passed the window frosted over with ice, the Christmas lights on the other side blurring into a sea of gold, red, and green. Outside, the soft moonlight set the snowy ground aglow; and I sighed at how beautiful it was.

There was something about Christmas Eve that seemed so magical. I didn't want it to go away.

"Melissa?" I turned at the sound of my name. Connor was standing by a row of glass shelves, holding up a Santa Claus doll. "What do you think?" He asked when he pushed the button in the back, and I laughed when a rap version of "Here Comes Santa Claus" began to play.

"That's ridiculous. Put it down." But my objection only seemed to encourage him.

"Well, in that case, I'll make you wait for your birthday—"

"If you buy that for me, I'm going to kill you." I jokingly threatened him, and he set it back where he had found it.

"Fine." He returned to me, wearing a clever smile on his face. "I'll find something else."

"You know, it's only a couple more days." I murmured and traced the face of a porcelain angel with my finger.

Whatever was coming—whatever all of this was leading up to, it wouldn't be long now.

"I know." He replied. "But you're forgetting something." I looked up at him, surprised.

"What?" I couldn't think of what it was.

"Mr. Oakman—how is he involved in this?" Connor asked as we moved on to the wooden tables, pretending to look at the snow globes. "This started happening in the fifties."

"He's eighty, now." I began. "So that would mean that he was twenty-one when April Lawson went missing." I lifted a globe up from the table and turned it over in my hands.

The base was white and heavy like limestone, and the snow that shifted inside sparkled like a handful of diamonds.

"But what about you?" He glanced at me, immediately returning his gaze to the table.

"He's a widower..." My voice trailed away as the thought suddenly occurred to me.

"Melissa," we fell silent when my mother called for me, and I turned my head in her direction, "I think I've found a winner." She stepped towards me, gingerly carrying something golden in her hands. When she drew closer, I realized it was an ornament gilded in filigrees and pearlescent swans; and it reminded me of a Fabergé egg.

"It's perfect." I nodded, agreeing with her.

"Great. I'll be at the check-out counter. Let me know if there's anything else you want to get before we leave." She said before walking back to the front of the store.

"I can't believe she's not your mom." He breathed, and I let out a sigh of my own.

"You and me, both." I drifted away from the snow globes and settled in the corner, where little boxes made of silver and frosted glass sat on wooden shelves on the walls. I lifted the lid of one of them, taken by surprise when "Carol of the Bells" began to play.

It was strange—how something that I once loved so much seemed so ominous now.

"Hey." I jumped, and the hand that had found itself on my shoulder pulled away. "I'm sorry." Caleb chuckled. "Did I scare you?"

"A little bit." I answered, my cheeks reddening in embarrassment.

"Well, it looks like it's time to take off." He stole a glance at my mother over his shoulder and smiled at the sight of his brothers carrying her things. "Did you find anythin'?" I withdrew my hand from the music box and brought it back to my side.

"No." I shook my head. "But it's fine. I don't need anything."

Why would I? In a week, I could be gone.
He wrapped his arm around me, speaking; and it was almost like he knew what I was thinking. But, of course, I was never good at hiding my feelings.

"It's Christmas Eve." He started as we walked down one of the aisles to doors. "You shouldn't be afraid to be happy." He turned to me, sincere. "Not even for a minute." I nodded. He was right.

"I won't."

"All right. Let's get in the car before the storm comes." My father called out to us, and we hurried out of the store and into the winter night.

"We strongly advise that you stay inside your homes. This blizzard has created some very dangerous conditions outside; but if you need to travel tonight, take extreme caution. We are anticipating that this storm will end tomorrow morning; but until then, stay tuned."

My father set the remote down on the table as my mother hastened down the stairs. I looked up at her from the couch, holding Tyler and Trenton close as if I could protect them from the storm that raged outside.

"I've straightened up the guest room for the boys, and I brought some pillows and blankets down if you two want sleep on our couches." She handed Connor and Caleb a pair of folded up comforters. "I'm sorry we can't take you boys home. Did you call your parents and tell them you're staying with us?" Caleb nodded in response.

"I called my mom as soon we got here." Connor replied.

"What do we do, now?" I wondered aloud, no doubt asking the question that everyone had on their minds; and my mother sighed, the sound masked by the sudden howling of the wind.

"Wait it out."

Gravel. That's what it sounded like. Gravel hitting my window again and again. And the wind—screaming relentlessly on the other side of my walls.

I sat up, unable to sleep, and wondered when it all would end.

Oh, I wished it would end.

But the hail kept falling, and the wind refused to stop. I stared up at the ceiling—at the stars that glowed light blue in the darkness.

I would never get to sleep this way.

I pushed the covers away from my legs and set my feet on the wooden floor, biting my lip when the boards creaked beneath my weight.

I slipped my pink fuzzy house shoes on; and pulling my robe over my shoulders, I turned the doorknob and tiptoed outside.

It was silent, except for the blizzard that ravaged the streets outside.

I stepped past the guest room and headed toward the stairs, immediately stopping in my tracks when I realized that the door was wide open.

"Trenton? Tyler?" I whispered their names, but no one answered. "Caleb!" I darted down the stairs in a panic and fell to my knees when I reached the couch pushed up against the wall. "Caleb!" I exclaimed as I laid my hands on his arm to jostle him awake. He jerked at my touch, and his eyes slowly fluttered open.

"Melissa?" He sat up when he spoke my name. "What's going on?" He twisted his face in confusion when he saw the terror in my eyes.

"Your brothers aren't in their room." I told him, and his own widened in surprise.

"What?" I moved back as he climbed off of the couch, walking briskly into the kitchen to look for them. "Tyler? Trenton?" I rose to my feet when he returned to the living room. "I don't know where they went." He breathed. "Do you think...?" His voice trailed away as he glanced at the front door; and I looked at him, suddenly terrified. Without a thought, I dashed to the door and threw it open, ignoring Caleb's shouts as I ran outside. "Melissa! You can't go out there by yourself!" He exclaimed as he raced after me, but I was already too far ahead. A gust of wind lashed at my face as I stood in the freezing cold, looking frantically around for them.

If they had gone outside, they couldn't have gotten too far.

"Trenton! Tyler!" I called out for them, my hair whipping around my head as the storm swirled around me; and the hail that fell from the sky clung to my clothes. Everything was so white; I could barely see anything in front of me. "Trent—" I started to cry out for them again, but a bright light caught my attention. I could only stand there, gazing at it in the stormy night. And I stole a step back when it drew closer, growing in the graying fog. A loud noise suddenly split the night in two—not the screaming of the wind—no.

It was something different—something else I recognized all too well.

I leapt out of the way as a white pickup truck sped down the road; and it screeched to a halt, the driver staring at me incredulously as he left his seat.

"Melissa? What were you doing in the middle of the street? I could have killed you!" The old man spoke; and at once, I wished I had stayed inside.

"Mr. Oakman..." His face softened, as if he'd realized how afraid I was.

"Are you all right?" He asked me. I stayed quiet, not really sure how to answer. But something rose inside me — and I wasn't sure if it was stupidity or determination.

"Chelsea Banneker..." I panted her name. "What happened to her?" His expression fell away from his face, revealing a solemnness I'd never seen in him before.

"Come with me..." He turned away from me and climbed back into the driver's seat; and against everything inside me that screamed for me to run away, I followed.

I stood in the doorway as I watched him drag his feet across the floor and sink into his armchair, shivering at the thought of what I'd done.

He was going to kill me — if he could. After all that happened, I wasn't sure if that was possible — killing a ghost.

"Are you coming?" I hesitated at his words, but closed the door and stepped inside. "Do you like stories, Melissa?"

"Depends on how they end." I answered, standing beside the couch that sat across from him; and he chuckled to himself.

"You're a clever girl." I stared at him as his voice slipped into an accent I couldn't distinguish. "Sit down. I think this one will interest you." I did as he asked, refusing to take my eyes off of him; and he looked down at the ground, losing himself in the darkness. "There was...a world where all things that have ever been imagined existed—*living, breathing creatures*. And in that world, eight kingdoms stood—forged in earth, air, water, fire, ice, wood, aether, and metal. The creatures walked the lands free—with wills and ambitions of their own; but the slaying of the most innocent of beings incurred an everlasting curse on the children of the earth, binding their souls with that of the creatures for all eternity. This continued for thousands of years until the world was stricken by great disaster: earthquakes, fires, blizzards, floods. It was not long before the inhabitants of those eight kingdoms realized that they were caused by people. This was strange, you see," he glanced up at me, "no one had ever gained power like that before, and no one ever would again. Threatened by their unexplained power, the others sent them away to a place beyond their reach—a place that they could call their own. And after six years, twenty-eight cities arose—each born from the marriage of two of the eight kingdoms; and in the city of earth and water, the first child of this disaster was born to the House of Torrowin, a noble family that hailed from the earth kingdom. But her mother, a former subject of the water kingdom, gave the child a name from the old language—a language, that when spoken by one touched by the Rytaronea, tears the veil between worlds itself."

"What was her name?" My voice trembled in my throat. And as he lifted his blue eyes from the floor, my heart stopped beating in my chest.

"Elynea Torrowin—the moon's shadow. Your mother—my daughter—she knew what you would become."

"But you said it was a story." I interrupted him, finding myself in a place far beyond my understanding.

I wasn't a ghost—I wasn't dead. I was something far more terrifying. And the man that I had lived all my years next door to had been watching me—protecting me.

"In every story, there is truth." He said simply, and I couldn't contest it. But then, another question came to mind; and I needed to know the answer.

"Why did they leave me here?" I asked him, desperate and confused.

"The curse of your father's people is in your blood. The creature meant to be your kindred spirit was chosen the day of your birth. But when your parents learned that it would be Kana'ti, they were afraid." He continued, but it only puzzled me more.

"Kana'ti?" I repeated; and he leaned forward, cautiously.

"He is a very dangerous man. Many have

died at his hands." I glanced down at my feet, wishing I knew so much more. "The day you turn sixteen is the day you must leave. He's been searching for you. And when he finds you, he won't let you go." I looked up at him, remembering Matthew's last words.

"No. I'll find him."

Chapter Eleven
Of Water and Earth

"Melissa! Wake up!"

"Wake up, Melissa!" I lifted my head up from my pillow, and the world slowly came into focus. Two little faces sharpened in front of me; and I sat up, rubbing my eyes as I yawned. Tyler and Trenton were standing at the side of my bed, waiting anxiously for me to join them. "It's Christmas!" Tyler exclaimed.

I remembered what that was like: waking up on the most magical morning of the year, staying up all night to see if Santa Claus had come to visit us yet, listening for the sound of hooves and sleigh bells on the roof. The place that I was really from—the fantastical place with no name—I wondered how much more exciting it would be, knowing that he was really coming.

"All right, all right." I said and glanced at

the clock on my nightstand.

Apparently, waking up first thing in the morning ran in the family.

I peered outside the window to my left; but all I saw was snow — snow and the wind that carried it past us. And I thought of the night before.

"Where did you two go?" I asked them; and they both shared a look of amusement, as if I had asked a silly question.

"We were looking for presents." Trenton replied as I stood, and I grinned to myself.

That made sense.

"You have a lot!" Tyler remarked as he grasped my hand, leading me out of my room and into the hallway.

"Wait, wait..." I slowed in my steps, whispering in hopes that we wouldn't wake the rest of the household. "It's too early." I told them when they stopped to listen. "No one else is up, yet."

"Well, that's not entirely true." I turned towards the voice and smiled as Connor emerged from the bathroom in his pajamas, rubbing the back of his ear with a facecloth.

"Hi." I spoke, inexplicably breathless; and he grinned, responding.

"Merry Christmas."

"Merry Christmas." It was strange — how only silence followed in that moment.

"Um, your mom's downstairs — if you

were looking for her." He stuttered and gestured to the stairs at the end of the hall. From where I was standing, I could see the amber light from the living room bleed onto the steps.

"Thanks." I answered and stepped in their direction, watching as the twins sprinted down ahead of me.

"What happened, last night?" He asked me once I was alone, and something inside me made me want to laugh.

"You wouldn't believe me—" I shook my head, but he kept me from finishing.

"I want to." He insisted; and in his eyes, I saw that he was trying to make sense of it all. "Ghosts, right? Newton's Third Law is completely applicable. When we die, we can't just stop existing—it would make sense that our energy would continue on in different forms. And when you drowned when you were a baby, your life force could have combined with the river's kinetic energy when you returned to your body or formed an entirely different being…" I listened to him as he rambled on, unsure of how to stop him.

Whatever he was saying, it seemed to be a reasonable explanation; but the truth—I didn't think science could explain that.

"I," it was difficult to admit, "I'm not a ghost." He paused, falling silent at my words.

"Then, what are you?" He wanted to know, and I opened my mouth to explain.

"Hey, Melissa." I whirled around to find Caleb standing on the steps behind me. The light emanating from downstairs cast a golden glow on his skin, and the sight of him caused me to run my fingers through my hair in an effort to fix it.

"Hi, Caleb." I said, beaming; and he caught me by surprise when he laid a kiss on my forehead.

"Oh, Connor…" Caleb looked up from my face, grinning when he saw him. "Merry Christmas." He nodded as he acknowledged him, and Connor buried his hands in his pockets as he did the same.

"Merry Christmas." I watched as Connor stole a step backward, as if he thought it'd be better if we were alone.

"Now that everyone is up, your mom was going to make some pancakes." He told me, and I placed my hand on his shoulder.

"I'll be down in a couple minutes." I glanced at Connor, adding, "I just have to brush my teeth."

"Sure." He replied and kissed the top of my head again before disappearing around the corner. I stood there for half a minute, just to be sure that he was gone, and turned to Connor once more.

"Come with me." I beckoned for him to follow me into my bedroom.

"What was that?" He asked me as I

pulled a piece of poster paper out from behind my desk and set it on the wooden surface. I sighed as I spoke, staring at the blank canvas that I had set before me. I silently gestured to the door, and he closed it behind him. "What's going on?" I looked at him, petrified; and he drew nearer to stand beside me. "What happened last night?"

"I woke up in the middle of the night and saw that Tyler and Trenton weren't in the guest room; and when I went out looking for them, I ran into Mr. Oakman." I finally said, and he stared at me incredulously.

"You're kidding."

"Or, rather, he ran into me." I wasn't sure which explanation was worse. "Or, he almost ran me over." Connor narrowed his eyes, and I could see the gears turning in his head.

"Wait, what?" He interjected when it finally registered in his mind.

"It doesn't matter." I insisted, continuing. "What matters is what happened after — when he got out of the car to see if I was okay, I asked him if he knew what happened to Chelsea Banneker."

"And he *didn't* kill you?"

If he hadn't revealed to me who he really was, it definitely occurred to me that he could have.

"Connor, he's my grandfather." He blinked at my response, and I repeated myself to make sure that he understood. "My *real* grandfather..." I retrieved a pencil from my desk drawer and began to draw out the crude outline of what I could only guess the other world could have looked like. "He told me I was born in another place—somewhere the things that we create with our imagination all exist." I drew an '8' on the left side of the map and wrote the list of elements beside it. "There are eight kingdoms, each representing a different magical element: water, fire, earth, air, ice, metal, wood, and aether. A long time ago, the earth kingdom was cursed to be bound to those legendary creatures; and a while after that, people all over the kingdoms suddenly became magical. He called it a name—'R'-something."

I wished that I'd remembered all that he had said.

"But either out of fear or hatred, the eight kingdoms sent all of them away so they could live apart from them." I sketched an arrow stretching from the left half to the other and drew a line that separated the land in two.

"So, a supernatural mass deportation— like the Trail of Tears or the Final Solution." Connor deduced; and for a moment, I hated myself for not realizing that sooner.

"Oh my gosh...I didn't even think about it." Everything in me seemed to droop and wither at the thought of it. It was heartbreaking—how even in two different worlds, human nature could still be capable of something so horrible.

"What happened next?" Connor nudged me to continue. I swallowed, regaining my focus.

"Twenty-eight cities were founded—all of them combinations of the eight kingdoms. And I was the first to be born in the city of water and earth." I set the pencil down next to all that I had written and gazed at it in disbelief.

The past month had made me question everything; and now, I finally had something to hold on to. But the truth—it wasn't at all what I had expected.

"My mother called me Elynea," the name felt so strange falling from my tongue, "but in the old language, it's spelled L-y-n." I stared up at him; and at once, he understood. "My mother was from the water kingdom, but my father's kingdom was the one that was cursed; so I inherited it, too. When my parents found out that the being that was meant to be bound to me was evil, they came here and tried to give me away so that I'd be safe; but it took a while before anyone really knew what my mother wanted."

"And so begins the legend of Crybaby Bridge." He whispered to himself. "But people have been seeing her for years."

"When someone magical speaks my name in the old language, it rips the veil however it wants." I tried to explain. "She couldn't control the time aspect, but she could make sure the door always opened in the same place. That's how my grandfather got stuck here in 1976."

"If this is true…" His voice trailed away, fading in his throat; and the thought that had found its way into his mind soon pervaded mine.

"He's been looking for me for sixty years…" I murmured. "He's just been taking the wrong ones."

Heather and Adrienne and Chelsea—I had no idea that he had been so close.

"We have to go back to the island on New Year's Eve. I can open the door, and you can take everyone home."

"What about Caleb? He's not coming with us?" I didn't answer, but the silence already told so much. "You're not telling him what we're doing, are you?"

"He already knows more than he should." I glanced down at my hands and saw that they were trembling. "Matthew didn't know anything; and he killed him, anyway."

"And what about you? We're all coming out of this, right?" He needed an answer, but his eyes pleaded for the one that I couldn't give him. But I grasped his hands regardless and forced a smile.

"Yeah. We'll get out of this."

"Okay, you guys. Smile!" My mother exclaimed as she held the camera before her face and snapped a picture. Immediately, the three of us were met with a flash of blinding light; and as I rubbed my eyes to chase the spots away, Connor let out a painful groan. "Oops! Sorry." She brought it closer to inspect it. "I left the flash on." Behind her, Tyler and Trenton battled each other with the plastic pirate swords that she had bought them the night before. Christmas music played on the radio sitting on the table, and the smell of chocolate chip pancakes lingered in the air.

"Mom, do we have to take pictures?" I asked her, both Caleb's and Connor's arms still draped over my shoulders.
Somehow, I had found myself in the middle; and I'd learned quickly that it wasn't something that I liked.

"Go ahead and open your presents. We can do group pictures later." She insisted and retreated back to the couch with my father, where he was waiting with gifts of her own. I sat down by the tree encumbered in ornaments and twinkling lights and waited for the boys to join me, but they both began to walk in the opposite direction.

"Where are you going?" I called out to

them; and Connor turned, suddenly sheepish.

"I was going to get a cookie." He gestured to the kitchen, but I beckoned him forward.

"Not all of these are mine." I told them, and they shared a look of confusion before kneeling by my side. "This one," I reached for the box wrapped in metallic green paper and handed it to Connor, "is for you. And this," I pulled a red gift out from underneath the tree, "is for you."

"Wow." Caleb breathed as he received it and leaned forward to kiss my cheek. "Thanks."

"You're welcome." I answered, blushing as I watched him tear the paper away to reveal a little brown box. He lifted the lid and set it down on his lap, and he grinned when he saw what lay inside. Carefully, he picked it up and held it to his eyes.

It was a leather cuff, a single iron charm dangling from it. And as he peered at it, I knew that he would see Orion wielding his bow and arrow, pointing it upwards as if to pierce the sky.

"From Moongirl," he chuckled a little as he read the tag aloud, "to Orion." The last word seemed to change him; and suddenly, there was something else in his voice—something that I didn't recognize right away. "Like the night we met."

Happiness…and nothing else. I missed that—more than I could describe.

"Should I go, next?" Connor inquired, and I nodded in agreement. "Cool." He said before he returned his attention to his own gift and stared at it, presumably guessing the identity of its contents. It was larger than most of the others, and I could tell that he was wondering what was inside. "Let's see…" His voice trailed away as he started to open it; and when he finally reached the interior of the white cardboard box, the laugh that left his lips said it all. He wrapped his fingers around the gift and pulled it out, shaking his head. "You…are… terrible." I couldn't help but descend into a fit of giggles as he gazed at me grudgingly over the red and white cap of the rapping Santa. "I hate you so much, right now."

"Look in the back." I encouraged him, but he brushed it off.

"Yeah, right. There's probably a fake spider in there." He commented, turning the silly present in his hands; but I persisted.

"Really. Look in the back." I reiterated; and with a hint of reluctance, he did what I had asked of him.

"Fine." He replied and opened the back. "What's this?" He looked up at me, awestruck at what I had given him. He pinched it with his fingers and held it up; and the Christmas lights reflected in the silver hands that grasped each other.

"Friendship rings." I spoke as I showed

him my right hand, its twin on my finger. "So you don't forget." His head perked up at my words; and instantly, I knew I had said too much.

"Forget what?" He began; and suddenly, a wave of silence washed over us.

It was eerie, so much so that it took me a while to realize that the music had also stopped; and the Christmas tree was consumed in darkness.

"Oh boy…" My mother whispered to herself, and Caleb's brothers stared up at the ceiling in surprise. "I guess what I was planning for dinner is out of the question."

"Uh…" I turned to Caleb when I heard his voice; and he shrugged, immediately making me uneasy.

He was always so sure of everything.

"Maybe not…"

"Thanks, Mom. Merry Christmas. I love you, too." Connor closed his phone and returned it to his pocket, turning to my parents. "She's doing all right. Mr. and Mrs. Richardson invited her over."

"Good. I'm glad she's not on her own." My mother sighed, standing. "Would you mind coming with me to the laundry room so we can take out some more blankets?"

"Not at all." He replied and left his seat

on the couch to follow her, leaving me alone in the blackness. I listened to Caleb and his brothers helping my father in the kitchen—or rather, my father telling the twins that his carving knives weren't toys, despite how cool they looked. I stared out the window and at the blizzard that continued on outside as night fell, filling the house with the shadows that came with it. I wrapped my arms around myself as I sat by the fire and closed my eyes, wishing that I hadn't seen what I had on Cedar Crest Island.

Because now, that was all I saw in the darkness: a black shapeless thing, drifting in a wind that shouldn't have existed, with a face—it was the face that terrified me the most—of an old man; but the image was so distorted, it was as if I were looking at it through a broken mirror.

"Hey." Caleb whispered, and the sound of his voice brought me back to the living room. He sat down beside me and gingerly placed a blanket over my shoulders. "I guess you're stuck with me for a little longer."

"This sounds like a terrible idea." I told him as I fixed my eyes on the Dutch oven sitting in the fireplace, the flames licking lazily at the sides. The smoky aroma of the ham baking inside filled my nostrils and wove itself into my hair and clothes.

"Come on," he responded, grinning, "they have whole websites for this kind of stuff. And besides, even if we set the place on fire, the alarm's not going to go off, anyway." I smiled to myself when he nudged me with his elbow; but in an instant, that smile was gone. "What's goin' on?" He asked me, but I didn't answer. "The way you were, this mornin'—there's somethin' wrong."

I hated how well he knew me.

"Can we wait—just for a little bit?" I stuttered. He nodded when he saw the look in my eyes and held me close.

"Sure. I'll wait as long as you want." He told me. "I'd do anything for you."

That's what I was afraid of.

Chapter Twelve

Hope upon Hope

"Elynea..." I whispered the name. "The moon and her shadow..." I gazed out the window and at the sky that traded its midnight blue cloak for a golden mantle and wondered.

If I could have stayed—if my mother hadn't given me away—what kind of person would have I woken up as? Would I have found myself in one of the many rooms in my family's palace? Would I have opened my eyes and seen the same stars that I saw now—but painted on the ceiling by the master illuminator? Or would I be lying awake, anticipating everything that my parents had planned for my sixteenth birthday?

My birthday. It suddenly occurred to me.

"Today's my birthday." I glanced at the door and then to my phone on my nightstand.

Connor—if there was anybody I wanted

to talk to, right now—six o'clock. I guess I'd have to wait another couple hours.

But as I laid my head back on my pillow, something white and square on the floor caught my eye; and I left my bed to step towards it. It was only when I drew closer that I realized that it was a note, and I bent down to pick it up. I squinted my eyes, unsure if I recognized the handwriting. "'Meet me in the backyard.'" The note requested, and I smiled when I turned it over and found a name written on the other side.

Orion

Quickly, I threw my robe on over my pajamas and slipped downstairs, passing through the kitchen and stopping by the glass sliding door to push back the blinds. And he was standing there, shivering as he stared up at the brightening sky with his hands in his pockets. He turned when I pushed the back door open and grinned.

"Hey, Moongirl." His voice speaking the name that he had given me sent butterflies fluttering through my insides, and I blushed as I stepped outside and into the snow.

"Hey." I breathed. "Why did you want to meet here?" Silently, he stole a step to the side; and I gasped at what had been standing behind him: a brass telescope—like the ones I had always seen in movies when I was younger—of the intrepid explorer who happens upon a band of pirates or of the eccentric astronomer and his much more grounded son. "Oh my gosh…" My voice trailed away as I carefully reached out to run my fingers across the cold surface.

It was so beautiful.

"You like it?" He asked, gazing at me expectantly. I lifted my eyes from the telescope to answer him.

"It's—it's amazing." I stuttered, still recovering from the surprise of it all.

"Good." I wouldn't get the chance. "It's yours." The smile fell from my face when he spoke.

"You're kidding…" I said, but the look in his eyes told me otherwise. "How did you…?" I started, but I couldn't finish.

"What's a moon without stars?" I looked up when he gestured to the sky. It was still thick with the gray clouds that had brought the storm our way, but I could see the light of the moon in silver streaks through the darkness.

The moon—it seemed so full already. I couldn't imagine what it would look like two days from—*oh*.

It didn't matter.

I turned to face him as he gazed up at the sky and saw him as I did that first night: the strange boy who had broken into my father's business just to let his brothers see the horses.

"Caleb?" I whispered, my voice trembling in my throat.

I was really going to do it. I was going to tell

him.

"Yeah?" His eyes lit up when he heard me call his name.

"I think...I..." It was hard to say. "These next few days—you shouldn't be here."

"Why not?" He took a step forward. Immediately, I regretted what I had said.

Whatever reason I gave him, he wouldn't leave me alone.

"My friend, Matthew..." I paused to find the words between the horrifying truth and what it would take to push him away. "It wasn't an animal attack." I watched as he wrinkled his forehead in confusion.

"Then, what was it?"

"I don't know." I shook my head. "I thought I was the only one who had seen it, but—but Matthew saw it too before he—" He placed his hands on my shoulders in an effort to quiet me.

"Whatever it is—whatever is goin' on, I don't care. I'm stayin'." He insisted. I bit my lip, angry at myself for only making it harder.

"I'm not asking." He brought his arms back to his sides, staring at my face with his dark brown eyes. He was searching for something in mine; and when his own widened, I knew that he had found it.

"You don't have to protect me." He knew me too well.

"I know."

"So why are you treating me like you have to?" I didn't want to answer. "Melissa."

I guess Moongirl was gone.

"Let me do this with you. I want to help." He raised his voice as he spoke, as if saying it louder would make me understand.

"I can't." I replied, and tears began to form in my eyes. "It's my fault. He's been looking for me. Like you said, I'm the only one who can do anything."

It was a scary thought. I was the only one.

"So you're going to martyr yourself?" He asked, and I wondered how clearly my intentions were set in the lines of my face.

Or if it was just another one of his gifts—looking at me and knowing my thoughts in an instant.

"Does Connor know?" I gazed up at him at the trace of jealousy in the mention of his name, fully aware of what my silence would tell him. But I was more preoccupied with the gravity of what I was doing.

He didn't know. And I intended on keeping it that way.

"You're forgetting that I've already been through this." He exclaimed. "Please, don't put me through it, again." He pleaded with me, but I couldn't let him convince me otherwise.

"I'm sorry." I stared down at my shoes and whispered; and when I looked up, the light that I had seen in him—that fleeting moment of happiness seemed to fade away before my eyes.

"So, this is how it ends?" He asked me, but the sudden realization was something that neither of us could escape from.

"This is how it ends."

A simple spark in the darkness—that's all it took to set them all aflame. Sixteen. It all seemed so real, now. The faces that surrounded me were suddenly illuminated in the flickering light, and I glanced at Connor sitting beside me. I never thought a day like this would feel so sad. Amidst all the singing and cake and presents, one single thought still lingered in my mind. And I couldn't tell them.

"Make a wish." I blinked as my eyes adjusted to the light of the candles and turned my head in my mother's direction.

"What?" I hadn't been listening. She gestured toward the cake that she had set before me. "Oh." The wax from the candles had already begun to drip onto the milk chocolate frosting. I held my breath captive in my throat and closed my eyes as I thought of what I wanted: to be back in the December of last year, when Heather and Matthew were inseparable—and when we were still too young to understand that we were nowhere near invincible. I blew them out; and all at once, their voices rang in my ears as they cheered and clapped their hands.

"All right," my mother spoke as she plucked the candles out of the frosting and set them down on a paper plate, "who wants cake?" I'd never seen Connor raise his hand so quickly.

I guess a year without cake every month had made him miss it.

I watched her slice a piece off of the corner and hand it to me on a plate.

"There you go."

"Thanks." I said when I received it, and my father placed the camera on the table.

"Sweet sixteen, huh?" He quipped, chuckling. "What are you going to do about that?"

I honestly had no idea.

"Um…" I started, but it seemed a lot harder to finish. Connor dropped his fork onto his plate at my silence and hurriedly answered for me.

"We have a list." I turned my head towards him as he continued. "Maybe we can knock off a few more places next year." He suggested; and I nodded, smiling.

"Yeah—sounds like a plan."

I stared up at the sky, watching as the stars sparkled before my sight, and drew in a deep breath of the chilly night air. The thunderstorms that had come with the blizzard left the atmosphere heavy with static; and as I breathed it in, it electrified my lungs. I looked out at the rooftops still covered in snow and grinned at the Christmas lights that had managed to cling to them through the storm.

"There you are." I heard my window slide open as Connor's voice carried out into the night, and I stole a glance over my shoulder as he climbed out of my bedroom and onto the roof. "It's about time for me to go home." He sat beside me and wrapped his arms around his legs.

"How was the rest of the party?" I asked him, smiling slightly.

I hadn't bothered to stick around.

"Boring." He exclaimed jokingly; and I stared at him, tilting my head to the side for a serious answer. "Really." He insisted. "It's not a party without Captain Sighs-a-lot." I shook my head at his words as he laughed. And then for a moment, it was silent as we both gazed at the night sky and the moon that had started to rise above the horizon. "It's like the calm before the storm—or," he paused to correct himself, "after the storm."

"The storm's just beginning." I murmured, just loud enough for him to hear me. "What do you think is going to happen—when all of this is over?" I looked at him, desperate that he'd abandon his practicality for a moment of irrational hope.

"I wish I could say that we'll go back to basketball games and having picnics by the lake, but I can't. I don't think it's ever going to be the same." My heart sank into my stomach, but I knew that he was right. "But I'll be there." He added, grasping my hand earnestly. "I'll always be there."

"Thanks." I lowered my eyes toward the frost-covered shingles, hoping that he wouldn't see the tears that had begun to stream down my cheeks.

"I got you something for your birthday." I looked up as he fumbled through his pockets and fished out a black velvet box the size of the palm of his hand. "I found it at the antique shop in Pryor." He said as a puff of mist escaped his lips.

It was strange—I'd forgotten how cold it was.

He opened it up, revealing a round silver locket inside, and took it out.

"Is it okay if I…" I nodded my head before he could finish, and he undid the clasp as I pulled back my hair so he could fasten it around my neck. "There." I blushed as he spoke inches from my face; but suddenly, his expression changed. And he wrinkled his forehead in surprise.

"What?" I reached for my hair, unsure of what he was seeing; and he pointed at something over my head.

"That." It was all he said. I lifted my head to find that the tears that had left my eyes were floating above me, and I laughed at the sight of him stretching his hand out to catch them. "You're so cool." He marveled; and as I watched him, another of Cedar Crest's mysteries was revealed to me.

And the one at the end of that long walk—I finally saw his face.

Chapter Thirteen
The Night Stared Back

$\mathcal{I}$ think there's a moment — that point when you realize what kind of person you want to be. It doesn't happen overnight. It starts — it builds — from the very second you take your first breath to the day you have to make a choice: between fighting for yourself and fighting for others.

And for me, I think today is that day.

I sat silently in my bedroom as I ran my fingers across the comforter covered in autumn leaves and smiled sadly.

My father had bought it for my seventh birthday. I remembered all the times Heather and I had turned it into a fort during our sleepovers — telling each other scary stories and pretending that we were damsels in distress. And the stars on the ceiling — somehow, my mother knew I'd like them before I even knew what they were.

I stood up from my bed and stepped toward the bedside table, taking a deep breath before pulling the drawer open and staring at what lay inside. The three of our faces gazed back at me as I lifted the picture frame from its place and set it back where it belonged. I turned my head as the doorbell rang, and my heart nearly stopped in my chest.

The time had come so soon.

"Melissa!" My mother called to me from downstairs. "Connor's here to pick you up for the party!" I buttoned my white trench coat over my maroon dress and touched the locket hanging around my neck — just to make sure that it was still there.

"I'll be down in a minute!" I opened my door to reply to her, suddenly startled when I found Connor standing in the hallway in his navy blue blazer and jeans. "Oh, hey." I felt the blood rising to my face as I spoke. "I'll be down in a minute." I repeated to him.

"You look nice." He simply said, and I couldn't hide the smile that crept its way onto my face. "You do know it's probably twenty degrees out there, right?"

Of course. There had to be a joke in there somewhere.

"I'll be fine." I insisted and reached for the light switch before closing the door behind me. I paused, afraid that it would be the last time.

"Melissa?" I looked up when I heard my name.

"Yeah?" I asked, my hand refusing to remove my fingers from the doorknob.

"Adrienne's expecting us." He glanced at his father's watch on his wrist.

He was right. We were already running a little late.

I nodded quietly and followed him down the steps leading into the living room where my parents waited on the couch. The New Year's Eve celebration in New York City was displayed on the television, and a bottle of champagne surrounded by a handful of glasses sat on the table.

"Have a good time, honey." My mother rose to her feet at the sight of me and held me tightly in an embrace.

"Thanks, Mom." I answered, immediately finding myself in my father's arms. "Love you."

"Love you, too." He responded as we parted, and Connor placed his hand on my shoulder.

"Are you ready to go?" He inquired expectantly.

"Yeah." I breathed, and we moved in the front door's direction.

"Melissa." I looked over my shoulder as my mother called for me, and the look on her face said more than she ever could. "Make sure you're home by 11:30." She told me, and I gave her the smile that she wanted.

"Sure." I unlocked the door and let Connor step out into the darkness ahead of me. And as I closed it, I took one last look inside.

"Are you coming?" Connor called from the front seat of his Oldsmobile; and hurriedly, I locked the front door, crossed the snow-covered lawn, and slid in beside him. His Letterman jacket was draped over the headrest of the passenger seat; and I realized that for a second, as fleeting as it was, I had forgotten what tonight was. For a moment, I stared through the windshield and up at the full moon that hovered above us. "So I guess this is how we're spending what could be our last night on Earth?" He joked, but I knew that he was just as terrified as I was.

"I guess it is." I replied, still gazing up at the sky; and without another word, Connor turned the key in the ignition. And Cedar Crest disappeared from view.

I didn't think that I would be standing at Adrienne Shelley's steps again. But somehow, I'd found myself there once more, as if time had fixed itself into a loop around me—always bringing me back to the place where I began. But this time, there was no game to be won, no trip across the state to see a haunted bridge in the middle of the night. Too much had changed since then for it to be that simple.

"You good?" Connor turned to face me as I reached out to press the doorbell, and I paused to answer.

"Yeah." I nodded and leaned on the button. Almost immediately, the door swung open, and Adrienne's bright blue eyes waited for us on the other side.

It surprised me, how alive she seemed compared to the corpse of her that we had seen in the hospital. But she was standing there, her golden hair falling over her shoulders as if the last few weeks had never happened.

"Hi, Melissa! Hey, Connor!" She exclaimed as she embraced me. "Happy New Year!" She rubbed her arms with her hands as she shivered in her gold sequin dress and ushered us inside. "Gosh, it's freezing out here. Come in." I shed my coat as I crossed the threshold, suddenly feeling the warmth that emanated from the fireplace. "I'm so glad you could come." Adrienne raised her voice over the music as she closed the door and took my coat to hang it in the closet to the left. "Follow me." She spoke as she grasped my hand. "Hannah and Chloe are here, too." I glanced back at Connor as I was quickly whisked away, but he could only grin before I was gone. We passed a table of cookies as she led me through the living room teeming with familiar faces, and I made a note to visit it again before we left.

It was so unusual for me—walking through a tunnel of people. I wondered how she could have possibly gotten used to it.

"Heads up!" A few of the boys from the basketball team called out, and I ducked just in time to avoid a box of pizza.

"Melissa!" I turned my head when I heard my name to see Dorothy in a pink dress, sitting at the piano as Melanie played something that sounded like it was from the seventeenth century; and I waved in response. We slowed as I spied Kris, Thomas, and Gregory on the couch in the living room; and Adrienne let go of my hand to stop and give Kris a kiss on the cheek.

"Hey, babe." She said, and he looked up at her with a smile. And in those blue eyes, I could see how much he loved her.

"Hey, Adie." Those blue eyes widened when he caught sight of me, as if he didn't expect that I would come.

I'd probably get a lot of that tonight. "Hey, Melissa. How's it going?"

"Great, thanks." I answered, but he held his hand to his ear to let me know that he hadn't heard it. "Great!" I said it louder, but he shook his head; so I gave him a thumbs up so he would understand.

"Oh! There they are." Adrienne chirped as Hannah and Chloe emerged from the kitchen with cups of soda and a bowl of chips, and she waved her arm over her head to claim their attention. The both of them beamed when they saw her, and they started to make their way from the kitchen and into the den. But Hannah paused when she caught a glimpse of me, and I watched as she whispered a few words to Chloe and walked into the living room instead. My heart sank into my stomach as Chloe shrugged sadly and followed her. "I'm sorry." Adrienne turned to me, apologizing. "I don't know what's going on with them —"

"It's okay." I shook my head, stopping her before she could finish.

So that's what everyone thought of me...How could they not? If I were anybody else, I would have thought the same thing.

It was all her fault. Melissa Moonwater — it was all her fault.

"I'll just go see what Connor's up to." I told her; and she nodded, frowning a little.

"Wait." She sighed when I started to leave, and I stopped to listen. "I know that you've been looking for Heather." And then I saw something — something she'd never shown me before. "Don't give up."

Hope.

"Thanks." I whispered, hugging her tightly; and I stepped away from the couch to return to the living room, hoping that Connor would be where I left him. But he wasn't. I stood on the steps by the front door in an attempt to find him among the crowd, scanning over the countless pairs of high school sweethearts cooped up in their own little corners, living life as if their microcosms were the only things that existed. My mind betrayed me, and I thought of Caleb—how much I missed him. But I pushed him out of my thoughts and reminded myself of what I had done—why I had done it.

Somehow, I knew: something terrible would have happened if he came with us.

"Hi, Melissa." I whirled to see Dorothy rise from her seat at the piano now occupied by a trio of girls trying and desperately failing to harmonize. "Happy New Year—" She corrected herself. "Well, not yet. We've still got a few more hours."

A few more hours. I wish I had more time.

She wrapped her arms around me, and I did my best to return the gesture. But when she let go, her lips had curved into a frown.

"What's wrong? Did something bad happen?" She asked, and I couldn't keep it inside any longer.

"I think I'm going to do something really stupid." I breathed, holding back tears that only showed themselves through my reddening ears instead. But the look on her face transformed into one of earnest encouragement, and it took me by surprise.

"Are you sure it's stupid? You don't really look like someone who would do something without a good reason." I opened my mouth to answer; but before I could, Connor was calling my name.

"Hey, Melissa." He began as he glanced at his watch. "I thought maybe we should take off a little early. You know, since we have somewhere else to go."

There he was again, trying to keep me safe from the troubled stares and worried whispers.

"Um…sure." I looked to Dorothy, with a head full of questions; but she had resumed her place at the piano, and "The Water is Wide" found its way into my ears.

"Are we just going to sit here?" I glanced at Connor as I asked him, but he continued to stare off into the distance — at the island that no longer seemed so far away. The air was still, the trees more silent than they'd ever been. A layer of ice had formed over the surface of the lake, and the light of the moon and the stars that surrounded it set the white plane aglow in the darkness.

"One more minute." He told me, and I knew what he was thinking.

This was really happening. "You know," he started, finally facing me, "we didn't think about the lake being frozen over." He grinned, and I couldn't help but smile too.

"I guess we didn't think about crossing it at all." I replied. And for one more moment, it was quiet as we gazed at Cedar Crest Island together. "Well," I rose to my feet and held out my hand to help him up from the ground, "let's get this over with."

"All right." He answered as he stood and followed me to the water's edge, and I sucked in the brisk forest air before setting foot on the ice.

"Here goes…" I took a step forward and immediately felt it crunch underneath me.

"Whoa!" Connor wrenched me backward as the ice cracked and buckled before our eyes; and the reservoir's water seeped up from beneath it, sending large sheets of ice floating over the surface. I looked at him, suddenly horrified.

"What do we do now?"

"I don't—I don't know." He shook his head. "If we tried to swim, we'd be dead before we got there." I turned my head away from the lake to face him at his words, and he scrambled to explain. "The water temperature of lakes covered in ice during the winter is about zero and four degrees Celsius." I blinked, not sure what he was saying. "Anywhere below fifteen degrees Celsius is immediately life-threatening." He shrugged, disheartened. "We can't cross it." I stared down at the water in despair and caught the silver reflection of the moon as it rippled, and I raised my face to the sky to feel its light on my skin.

"Maybe we don't have to." I whispered and glanced down at my hands.

If I could concentrate hard enough— maybe I could do it.

I shut my eyes and wished for what I wanted.

For Heather.

All at once, something surged through me, as if I had been struck by lightning; and it tickled my insides and branched out into my hands, finally settling in my fingertips. I opened my eyes to see them shrouded in a bright white light, and I gazed at them in amazement.

"Melissa…" Connor murmured, tapping me on the shoulder; and I lifted my eyes and set them on the water. The surface began to shift, bubble almost; and as I squinted my eyes, I gasped as I realized what was happening. Like fireflies in the night, droplets of water illuminated by the moon drifted up into the air and filled the darkness with a thousand stars. "That's all you, isn't it?" He marveled, and I could only nod in response. Silently, I moved forward; and he leapt in front of me to keep me from getting any closer. "Wait. What are you doing?" He asked, knitting his brows together in concern; but I grinned in response.

"This is how we're getting to the other

side." It was all I said, but it was enough to convince him. I stepped down into the lakebed and felt my boots sink an inch into the mud.

I guess I still had to learn a few things.

"What about the..." His voice trailed away as his answer floated over his head in the form of a fish trapped in a globe of suspended water. "Well, okay..."

"Connor, hurry!" I called to him, already farther down the path. "I don't know how long this will last."

"Right." He sprinted after me, suddenly stopping when he saw the look on my face. "What's going on?"

I'm not sure he wanted to know.

"Come here..." I gestured frantically, lowering my voice.

"Sure." He answered, raising his eyebrows a little as he took a step forward. "Are you gonna tell me what's going on?" I held my breath, my heart losing a beat with every step that he took towards me.

He didn't see it.

Even in the darkness, it seemed to thicken the night with a blackness that couldn't be quenched with the moonlight. That thing that I had seen the night that Matthew died — the being cloaked in shadows — hovered a few feet from the ground, staring at me with its frighteningly black voids for eyes. It stayed there, unmoving, as silent as Death itself as it gazed at me. The tips of its robe dispersed like tendrils of smoke that curled around its body and masked most of its face, but I knew that I could never forget what I had seen.

"Okay." Connor spoke when he was standing by my side. "I'm here. What's going on?" When I didn't respond, he turned to face the direction in which I was staring; but he scratched his head in confusion. Without a sound, it moved closer; and I stole a step backward, closer to the island.

"Connor?" I said his name, never taking my eyes off of the monster that slowly glided towards us.

"Yeah?" He replied, looking all about him as if he knew that he was missing something.

"You're going to have to run." I breathed, terrified as the space between us and the being grew smaller and smaller.

"What?" He asked, dubious; but when I locked eyes with him, he knew that I was serious.

"Run!" I shouted one last time as the phantom sped down that path with a bloodcurdling shriek of its own; and I crossed my arms in front of my face as water suddenly came rushing at me at all sides, and I lost my footing as it carried me away. I tumbled around in the murky water, the current pulling me in every direction but up; and I flailed my arms over my head and toward the sky to no avail.

What felt like a million needles pierced my skin and set my limbs on fire; and even as I tried to scream, the breath was left frozen in my lungs. My whole body ached, cried out to make it stop; but all I could do was sink paralyzed into the darkness. With heart racing and lungs burning, I attempted to gasp for air and swallowed water; and my insides screamed in agony. And as the world darkened before me in the dizzying cold, I knew that this was what it was like to die.

"Melissa! Melissa!" Hands—trembling hands. It was hard: dragging me onto the bank. I couldn't move, couldn't speak. It was still so cold. "Please. Please don't die on me." My chest hurt, like my ribs had been broken in the struggle. "You're not done! You have to save Heather! We have to save..." Scattered breaths, and something else—I couldn't determine what it was. The smell of mud filled my nostrils; and for a moment, I saw the stars above me. But they blurred and blacked out as quickly as they had appeared. "Melissa! Melissa—come on! Come on..." Everything went numb: my fingers, my arms, my legs—and the pain in my chest, it was gone too. "I love you. You hear me? I love you..."

Chapter Fourteen

Moonshadow

My eyes fluttered open as I took my first breath, and the taste of smoke took hold of my tongue. I coughed it out of my system as I sat up, and the world came back to me as I gathered my senses. Trees. I was surrounded by trees, and the snow had been pushed away from where I had been lying. Disoriented, I turned my head toward the fire that flickered in the pit beside me; and the outline of a young man crouching by the flames disappeared from view.

"Melissa!" Connor breathed as he scrambled on his hands and knees to my side, and he placed his hand on my shoulder. "Are you okay? Oh gosh, I thought you were gonna die." I grimaced as I set my hand on my forehead, shivering.

So did I.

"Let me get you something." He hurried to a tree limb laden with our coats and grasped his Letterman jacket; and when he returned, he gingerly draped it over my shoulders.

And I remembered seeing Adrienne sitting atop her desk in History class, wearing Kris' jacket over her shoulders—like I was wearing his.

"You have to go." I whispered to him, continuing before he could protest. "I need to do this by myself."

"You almost died back there." He quickly glanced back at the lake far behind us. "What do you think would have happened if I didn't come with you?" I couldn't answer. "And besides, there's no way to get back anymore."

He was right. I could try to make a pathway again, but there was no guarantee that I would be able to.

"I'm in this now. There's no getting rid of me."

"You didn't see what I saw. This is real…" I breathed. "When my grandfather told me that everything that's been imagined really existed, he meant everything—even the monsters." I told him, eyes wide.

"That doesn't scare me." He insisted, with one last spark of skepticism in his eyes.

"It should." I responded, but he looked down at the toothed edges of the zipper on his jacket. He was still holding them.

"Then I guess I'm not as smart as you think I am." He pulled me closer to him with the edges of his coat until the space between us was no more, and our lips met in a kiss that seemed to have been waiting longer than we could have ever known. It obliterated everything else around us; and in that moment, I forgot where I was. It wasn't electric—not the way it felt when Caleb and I first touched. It was more than that—the only proof I needed to know that magic really existed. I couldn't keep myself from blushing when we parted, and the blood was rushing so loudly in my ears that I could barely understand what he said next. "Why did I wait so long?"

"I'm asking myself the same thing." I chuckled in the silence. But we would have to answer that question later. "How long has it been?"

"What?" I'm sure to him it seemed to come out of nowhere.

"What time is it?" I asked him; and he checked his wrist, taken off guard when his watch wasn't there.

"Hold on." He hurried to the other side of the fire pit and plucked his watch up from the ground. He paused when he held it up to his face. "Two and a half hours—it's 11:51…"

"We need to get going." I tossed his jacket to him over the fire as I stood and sprinted to the tree behind him to retrieve my coat.

"Wait!" He exclaimed and kicked a heap of snow onto the flames, leaving the embers sizzling underneath the wood as they died. "Going where?" He wanted to know.

"The last time we were here, I found a tree." I paused in my frantic scramble to glance back at him. "We have to get to it before midnight." Connor stared at me, and his face said it all.

"How are you going to find a single tree in a place like this?" He gestured to the countless trees that surrounded us.

It was a valid question, but it didn't matter. We had to make it.

"Follow me." Immediately, I hurried through the woods, toward the clearing where we had pitched our tent only a week or so before; but when I reached it, something made me stop.

"What is it?" Connor slowed in his steps when he caught up with me, but I was silent.

There it was, again — that feeling — pushing me forward.

Slowly, I wandered through the trees, losing myself in that feeling. It called for me, and I couldn't stop myself from walking towards it. Suddenly, a strange breeze caught itself in my hair.

And I knew.

The pine tree towered over us like a giant, dressed in a mantle of emerald leaves. It stood, solemn, and still so frightening in the moonlight that draped its bark in silver. It seemed so much more mystical, now — as if the full moon's presence unlocked its secrets.

"This is it, isn't it?"

"Yeah." I murmured, speechless. It beckoned me forward as it had before, and I took a step across the ground covered in leaves long dead. A faint whisper found its way into my ears, multiplying as I drew closer. "Do you hear that?" I looked over my shoulder at Connor, but he shrugged in disappointment. I returned my eyes to the tree, widening them as a glittering curtain of foreign symbols materialized before me. Golden letters of a language I'd never learned — they sparkled in the darkness; and I blinked to be sure of what I was seeing.

"Whoa." Connor simply said, and I turned to face him.

"You can see it?" I asked him in amazement; and he nodded, dumbfounded.

"What are they?" He inquired as he joined my side. I peered at them, trying desperately to discover their meaning; and as if they sensed my presence, they rearranged themselves, breaking up into pieces and forming into something else — something I could understand.

"They're words..." I opened my mouth to speak them, but a loud crack in the distance shattered the quietness; and we locked eyes before searching the shadows that threatened to devour us on every side. Something darted through the blackness, and the silhouette of a man came hobbling to us as quickly as it could.

"Mr. Oak—I mean, Grandpa..." I sighed at the sight of him. "What are you doing here?" He paused to catch his breath, bending over to place his hands on his knees.

"I knew you would come. You have to understand what's waiting for you on the other side." He pleaded with me as he coughed; and Connor ran to him to make sure that he was okay. "You can't go, Elynea. You can't fight him." He shook his head. "Even if you manage to rescue your friends, he won't let you return with them." I gazed at him sadly and then glanced back at the golden letters; but somehow in that time that they had transformed and when he had appeared, they had faded away until they were nothing at all.

"I'm not leaving them." I started. "If I have that chance to bring them back, I'm going to take it." I turned to Connor; and I knew from the look in his eyes that despite his own reservations, he understood.

"Don't worry. I'll stay behind with him." He promised me, but something told me that waiting was the last thing he wanted to do. "Just come back, okay?" Wordlessly, I stepped in his direction, breaking into a run halfway through, and wrapped my arms around him.

"I will." I let go, knowing that if I held on any longer that I wouldn't be able to; and I looked up at the moon one final time.

"Your mother would be proud of you, but your grandfather is allowed to worry until you return." My grandfather let his concern overshadow his smile as he shook his head and embraced me; and for the first time, I knew what home was really like. I hurried to the tree again, and the ancient letters revealed themselves once more. Closing my eyes, I drew in a deep breath and spoke.

"Moonshadow —" At the sound of my voice, the veil was torn open; and a great gust of wind came surging at me from a place that I couldn't see. The curtain of golden words burst into a million tattered pieces, falling away in a shower of shimmering flames. I covered my eyes to shield them from the light, but it was brighter than any sun could have ever been. And then, it was gone; and I was left standing in the darkness of the forest.

"It didn't work." I whispered to myself; and as my vision blurred, I knew that it was the tears that came to my eyes. "Connor," I turned to face him, "it didn't…"

But he and my grandfather were gone,

and only silence took their place.

"Connor?" I called his name once more, but something told me that he was too far to hear it. I stole a step backward, my wet shoes squishing against the cold hard ground; and I stared at it in confusion.

Where had all the leaves gone?

Cobblestones paved the sylvan floor in their stead, and I lifted my eyes to see that they formed a path underneath my feet and led somewhere farther up ahead. It was quiet, save for the warm breeze that rustled through the tree branches.

And I remembered. It was summer here.

Absentmindedly, I took off my coat and followed the road, glancing at the trees around me.

They didn't look any different.

But suddenly, a fleeting glimpse of moss green skin darted from one trunk to another; and I quickened my pace. An amber light burning just outside the forest came into view, and I raced towards it anxiously, pausing as I came to the end of the wood.

If I had ever been to Paris, I imagine it would have looked like this.

Gothic arches graced the façade of nearly every building, and towers and domes of glass touched the clear night sky. It seemed that not a soul was awake tonight, leaving the magical place in its entirety for me to explore. A great river split the ancient city in two; and a large stone bridge crossed over it, making it whole again. Hesitantly, I set foot on the bridge, afraid that it couldn't possibly be real; but it was, and I ran my fingers along the filigrees engraved into the railing. I looked down when the details at the base of the bridge caught my eye, only to find that the phases of the moon hovering over a herd of wild horses had been carved into the stone.

The city of earth and water—I was here. I was home.

The river gurgled beneath me, and I stole a glance over the edge of the bridge in time to catch a glimpse of a glass boat gliding across the surface of the river. I blinked in wonder as I watched its occupant row it to a submerged floor of one of the buildings and saw that it was glass as well; and he unlocked an iron gate and drifted out of sight.

"Wow." I sighed. My grandfather never told me how beautiful it was; but then, he hadn't seen it in more than thirty years.

I gazed up at the starry sky and gasped as I witnessed the constellations take shape and dance above me.

Orion in all his glory lit up the darkness as he taunted the Great Bull; and Taurus charged at him, huffing in a rage when the Hunter evaded him and sent the seven Pleiades scattering in the other direction. In the quietness,

I laughed a little to myself and rested my chin on my hands as I watched.

"The stars are different here." I lifted my head at the voice, eyes wide.

"You."

Chapter Fifteen

Apples and Toffee

"Hey, Moongirl." He stood at the other end of the bridge and smiled, brown eyes sparkling.

It was so odd—he didn't look out of place at all.

"Caleb…" I whispered his name as he strolled towards me with his hands in his pockets, and the fires in the streetlamps seemed to brighten as he walked past. "Did you follow me here?"

Something told me that I already knew the answer.

"No." He shook his head with a grin, but it fell from his face when he saw how perplexed I was. "I'm here to take you home." He held out his hand, but I could only stare at it. "It's okay." He reassured me, and I placed my hand in his and let him lead me to the other side. He stopped at what I had previously believed to have only been a pillar; but as he placed his hand on the stone wall, it caved into itself, revealing a narrow flight of stairs spiraling down to the water. I glanced at him, uncertain. "Go on." He gestured for me to enter; and when I didn't step inside, he took the lantern from the staircase wall and led the way.

"You're from here?" I spoke, looking back as the wall closed us in; and I learned quickly that I had claustrophobia.

"Yes." He turned his head to face me as he waited on the bottom step. "I've lived in Xaijena for a while, now."

Finally — a name.

"Xaijena?" I repeated. "Is that where we are, now?" I asked him when I reached the end of the staircase.

"This is Rynmoor. Xaijena is what they call the twenty-eight cities as a whole." He replied and opened the door, and a wave of mist came wafting over us. My heart fluttered in my chest when he left the hollow pillar and stepped aside, revealing another gondola made of glass docked at the edge of the platform. He closed the wooden door when I emerged from the tower; and I stepped closer to the transparent vessel to run my hand along the side, leaving a glowing handprint wherever skin and glass met. I was startled when it suddenly bobbed in the river, and I looked up to find that he was already sitting in it. He beckoned for me to join him, and it rocked slowly when I climbed inside. I sat across from him, holding my legs tightly with my arms when he reached for the oars and began to push us away from the bridge and down the river. I averted my eyes when he glanced at me, but it wasn't enough to escape his attention. "You're wondering why." He said as we passed the building that I had seen before, and I gazed down at the water to realize that all of them stretched down below the surface with walls of enchanted glass. "I just wanted to meet you—before it came to this." He lifted his head to gaze up at the arches above us; and for a second, I saw him as who I thought he was the night that we met.

"What made you stay?" I wanted to know.

"I didn't know that you grew up in the dark about this place—about yourself. And when the Wendigo attacked your friend—" He began, but I had so many questions.

"A Wendigo killed Matthew?" I interrupted him, but he didn't seem to mind.

"No. The shadow creature that you saw that night—what we call a Ravenmocker—that's what killed him. It preys on the weak and the dying. It's been following the Wendigo for a while now." He answered. "As a daughter of the water kingdom, you inherited a healer's blood— the only thing that they're afraid of. You wrote the Ravenmocker's death sentence when you saw it, but I couldn't determine who the Wendigo was in time."

"What do you mean?" I wrinkled my forehead, concerned.

"They can assume any shape they want. It could have been anyone." I peered at him at his response, and he chuckled lightly. "It's not me. They can't stay in human form too long before they need to hunt."

I believed him. I'm sure I would have noticed a monster sleeping on the couch downstairs.

I took in my surroundings when the boat floated into the mouth of an underground tunnel lit with torches fastened to the walls and drifted through an invisible barrier that shimmered with silver when it touched my face.

"What was that?" I looked back at it over my shoulder as we slowly glided away, deeper into the heart of the city.

"Only a Torrowin can enter this part of Rynmoor." He said as we came to a series of smaller arteries of the river, and he rowed the boat through the second to the right. Candles in place of torches lined both sides of the narrow cave and filled the watery path in little white ceramic bowls, their firelight setting the water aglow as the bow of the gondola pushed through them. I opened my mouth to ask him why and what that would make him in relation to me; but as we came upon the end of the tunnel, those words left my throat before I could speak them. An underground garden, with arches that mirrored those of twice the size outside carved into the rocky dome walls—and massive trees laden with a myriad of magnolias giving shade to pools of the bluest of water. I glanced up at the ceiling and found that it was covered in a million living stars that sparkled as they drifted over my head and illuminated the cave. We came to a stop at a patch of grass, and Caleb leapt over the side and held out his hand to pull me onto solid ground. I stepped into the center of the garden and placed my hand on the trunk of the tallest magnolia tree, careful not to stumble over the circle of tiny stones that surrounded it. All five of the trees seemed to be guarded by them, and I marveled at the sight.

"Why did you bring me here?" I whirled to face him, and he looked down at the ring of rectangular stones by my feet. I drew closer to them, and my heart sank into my stomach when I realized what they were. Headstones. All of them. "You said you were going to take me home…" My throat hurt as I swallowed, and my eyes began to fill with tears.

"Melissa," it was hard to say, "you've been gone for two hundred years." He took a step towards me; and I backed away from him, shaking my head.

"No…You're lying…" I felt the magnolia

tree against my back and knew that there was nowhere else to go.

"Melissa…" He reached out his hand to comfort me as I looked at them again; but this time, I saw something that I hadn't seen before.

"Why did they die on the same day?" I asked him, horrified; and he returned his attention to the markers with a somber look on his face. "You know, don't you?" I called his name when he didn't answer. "Kana'ti…please…" At once, he turned to me, the sadness drowning the fire in his eyes. "Did you kill them?"

"No…" He told me, a deep sorrow falling from his lips; and I thought of the woman that he loved before.

Had he told me the truth then? Or did he kill her too?

"Why don't I believe you?" I wanted to — so much; but my mind told me that I couldn't, and it was enough. I glanced down at the nearest pool of water and wished to be home again — whatever that meant, now. With Heather and the others and then back to Cedar Crest — back to Connor and my parents and my grandfather. To the family that I still had.

"Melissa, no—" He shouted as I gathered as much air as I could into my chest and dove into the water that wasn't as shallow as it appeared to be, and his muffled words faded away the deeper I found myself. It seemed endless—that pool of water; but there was no clear way out of it, and I panicked as I fought to keep the same air in my lungs.

I couldn't return to the surface—he would be waiting there for me. But staying in the water only to drown frightened me more.

I broke the face of the pond, terrified of what awaited me on the other side; but as I dragged myself over the edge, a cold hard floor caressed my skin. I coughed up water as I lay on the tiles, disrupting the quiet that shouldn't have greeted me at the surface. I lifted my head up from the floor and saw the moon through the skylight, and I knew that I was somewhere else. I pulled myself up from the ground, my drenched dress weighing me down; and I gathered my senses in this new place. A crystal chandelier hung from the ceiling, but it gave no light. It left the room in utter darkness—save for the silver light of the moon that reflected in the water and mother of pearl that covered the wall behind it. I shivered and held my arms before leaning against the wall, and I turned my head to the right to see that the room narrowed into a long corridor with a pair of two silver plaited doors at the end. Silently, I walked towards it, trembling all the way down the hallway; and I hesitated at the doors, not sure if I wanted to push them open. But when I curled my fingers around the metal handle, I knew that I had no other choice. With a creak, the heavy doors gave way. White gossamer curtains fell over the windows from frames of twisted silver, reminding me of the sign at my parents' ranch; and the ceiling—the ceiling was painted with the constellations of the winter sky. It was...almost magical—how closely it mirrored the sky I had seen not too long ago. It was empty, like the room before; but white wooden dressers stood near the western wall. And a mahogany chest sat at the foot of a bed canopied in periwinkle drapes. Desperate for dry clothes, I hurried to the chest and lifted the lid; and a mass of royal blue fabric met my eyes. I peeled my maroon dress from my skin and set it aside, slipping the new gown over my head and letting it fall just inches from the mosaic floor. I found my reflection in a mirror situated in between a pair of windows and traced the silver metal fashioned into lace panels at my right hip and left shoulder in curiosity.

"It's funny—that you would pick that one." I jumped at the sound of another voice and turned to face a little girl no older than ten in a white nightgown. She gazed at me with hazel eyes, her long black hair cascading just below her shoulders.

"Hi..." I couldn't think of anything else to say.

"Why are you here?" She asked me, but the animosity that I expected was replaced with interest instead.

"Why are *you* here?" The bedroom seemed to belong to someone else—the dress couldn't be hers.

"I was looking for Jistu…" She gestured to something much lower to the ground behind me; and a brown and white hare leapt out from underneath the bed and into her arms.

"Your rabbit?" It sounded like a strange name for a pet.

"He's not a rabbit." She replied, and I opened my mouth to ask her what she meant.

"Norrie?" A woman in her early thirties wandered in through the doorway, immediately holding her daughter behind her at the sight of me. "Who are you?" I scrambled for an answer, not really sure how to respond.

"Melis—Elynea. Elynea Torrowin." At my words, she took a step towards me and narrowed her eyes as she stared at my face—as if she were looking for the truth. They suddenly widened when she found it, and she marveled at the gown that I had stolen from the chest.

"Welcome home, lost one."

"Has it really been two hundred years?" I sat across from her in the study as Norrie sat in her lap; and from the corner of my eye, I watched a young man bend down in front of the fireplace and set the wood ablaze with a whisper. He wore different colors than the others: a red tunic and leather blackened with soot. The woman nodded sadly, and I sighed in frustration before raising a goblet rimmed with silver moons to my lips. Its contents warmed my insides, flooded my mouth with the taste of spiced apples and toffee; and instantly, I was filled with an agonizing longing for Mrs. Harrison's Thanksgiving pie.

"They called you the Lost One—the only one of the Morkoa to never come of age and lead her people." She replied solemnly, furrowing her brow in confusion when she saw the look on my face. "You don't know?" I shook my head no, and she patted Norrie on the back and spoke. "Xeanora, you know which book to take, yes?" The little girl nodded and slid off of her mother's lap to pull a rather large tome from the shelf of a bookcase that replaced the wall to my right.

There were so many of them—I could spend a year in this room and still not finish them all.

"Beautiful name." I commented before she returned.

"She was blessed with all three gifts of this city. I thought it only fit to honor the one of the Thirteen who made it so." She glanced at me and then back to the child who placed the book on the table between us.

"The Thirteen?" She smiled, amused at my question, and set her hand on the leather binding.

"You have a lot to learn." I stole a glimpse of the cover of the book before she began to flip through its pages.

What the Gods Have Given

Those golden words appeared to have lasted a great deal of time, evident through the worn leather and yellowed parchment tucked inside. She paused at a page with the word that she had spoken before written in calligraphy.

"Read this." She encouraged me, turning the book over so I could read it.

"The Morkoa: the first twenty-eight children born from the Rytaronea, or Great Rift, believed to have been the most powerful beings to exist in this world in exception to the Thirteen Gods of Old." I started, in awe of the first sentence that I read aloud. "With dominion over all forms of magic, they governed the cities of Xaijena, the most notable the seven born to the cities of the elements and Rift: the purest of magic — and the most chaotic. Though not among the ranks of Cerelene Haberath the Invincible and Kaliveia Endymor the Gentle, the name of Elynea Torrowin the Lost is known in every city, due to the mystery surrounding her existence. Rumored to have been born to the Torrowin family in late 1827, she disappeared not long after, leaving her descendants with no

Legacy to call their own. Her gift, which can only be assumed to have been over the moon itself, has since never been discovered." I lifted my eyes up from the page when I was finished, left with almost no words to say. "This is me?"

Why hadn't my grandfather told me this? But then, if he had, I would have found a way here sooner.

"The Morkoa were like gods in their time—endowed with great power. When they passed from this life, their descendants were able to draw from them when in need of a strength that they couldn't possess themselves. That's why we have Rathon." She gestured to the young man sitting far too close to the flames, and I noticed that the heat didn't seem to bother him at all. "The city of Jaza has been sending soldiers to protect the Torrowin family for two hundred years."

"So you…" She nodded her head before I could ask her the question.

"Paia Torrowin—her father," she looked back at the fireplace where Norrie had joined Rathon; and he reached his hand into the fire to retrieve a finch with iron feathers that took flight around the room, "Alyus, and her brother Mysric are travelling to the capitol to convene with representatives from the other governing families; but they should be returning in the next few days."

It suddenly came to me, and I wondered

why I hadn't realized it before. I had wished to be with the only family I had left—and found myself here.

"Do you know...what happened to my parents?" She gazed at me sadly, and I wasn't sure if I wanted to know anymore.

"Legend speaks of a monster that feared your connection to Kana'ti. It believed your partnership would mean the end of many of the evil spirits that roamed these lands. But when it came to murder you in your crib, you were already gone." She sighed.

"So it killed my family instead..." My eyes burned as I spoke, and I lowered them to stare at the rings in the wooden table. "*That's* why you have Rathon."

"Few escaped—only by the combination of their power of earth and water—through tunnels that they created under this house and throughout the city. One of them being your aunt Halaei—an ancestor of ours." I looked up at the sound of her name.

I would have given so much to meet her. Hear her voice—and listen to the stories about my mother.

"What were my parents' names?" I couldn't keep myself from asking. I wanted to know. More than anything.

She smiled.

"Lyrand and Nyanna." They sounded so familiar—so safe. Like the very names wrapped themselves around me and held me close. "You can stay here—if that's what you want." I grinned at the thought of it: staying in Rynmoor. But I couldn't.

"I came here to find my friend. She was taken from the world I grew up in almost a year ago. Do you know how I might be able to find her?" I inquired, and her kind brown eyes showed me that she understood.

"You came to us through the reflecting pool?" She laughed a little at the face I made. "I followed the trail of water. The gift you have— it's not uncommon; but it is difficult to control. Master that, and you can transform any body of water into a door to what you seek." She paused. "It may take a while, but I can show you."

"Thank you." My vision began to blur— Paia's face and the countless books behind her head bled together before my sight. And I couldn't determine if it was from exhaustion or the tears that must have gathered in my eyes. But there were no tears. Only the heaviness that pervaded the muscles in my limbs.

"Come with me." She insisted, standing; and I pushed back in my seat to rise with her. But my knees weakened, and I reached out my hand to steady myself against the table—only for my fingers to collide with the stem of the empty goblet and send it rolling onto floor.

"Sorry." I exhaled, feeling the heat of the blood rushing to my cheeks. My ears. My head.

And I crouched down to rescue the vessel from where it had landed. But the last of my strength gave way to the numbness that overwhelmed my senses — held my body for ransom; and my hand slipped from the surface of the polished wood.

Chapter Sixteen

On the Other Side of the Door

$\mathcal{I}$ opened my eyes to darkness, to nothing but a black expanse unending around me; and the paralyzing fear that I was dead took hold and couldn't be dispelled. But I was breathing. I could feel my chest rise and fall as the air filled my lungs. And a dull ache seized my body as I returned to consciousness, and I knew.

This wasn't Death.

"Paia?" My voice cracked in my throat as I called her name into the void. "Paia?" I waited in the quiet for an answer. But there was none. I squinted, hoping that my eyes would adjust to the dark; but no object came into focus. No outlines sharpened to set themselves apart from the all-consuming shadows. And I fought to recall what had brought me here.

The smell of old paper and ink. The

flicker of embers on a sparrow's wings. Warm apples and toffee.

It was the last thing that I remembered, and yet—the taste had turned bitter on my tongue.

I pushed myself up from where I had been lying to discover that my hands sank into the material beneath me, and something soft slipped away from my shoulders to expose my skin.

Connor's jacket.

I half expected to hear his laugh—blink and find myself sitting alone in his car in Kellyville. But that reality was gone.

I held my fingers before my face and shook them gently in an attempt to light them like a match, and they sparkled briefly before falling dim once again.

"Come on. Come on." I muttered underneath my breath. "Your power is literally in your name." I bit my lip as I reclaimed my focus and directed it into both of my hands, the muscles wrapped around my bones warming as the gift I called to life began to rise inside me. My mouth ran dry as the heat intensified, burning white hot at my fingertips. And five bursts of moonlight erupted like fireworks into the darkness. It illuminated the room in an instant, dipped the walls and bedposts in silver; and I examined my surroundings before the light dimmed into a moderate glow.

I'd been here before. The ivory bureaus, the pale blue canopy, the stars that shimmered faintly overhead — the memory of them was fresh in my mind, but a feeling of some deeper familiarity refused to abandon me.

I'd seen this place long before tonight.

An object to my right caught the light I had conjured and reflected it just within the boundaries of my sight, and I brought my hand over the bedside table to dissolve the shadows. It was an elaborate tube of silver securing a roll of parchment. Reliefs of twin horses underneath a full moon appeared to race into life from the confines of the metal. Their muzzles met in a sapphire kiss, the gem glittering like a drop of water on a mirror. Succumbing to my curiosity, I liberated the paper from its safeguard and unfurled it to gaze at the words scrawled almost frantically in a troubling message; and my lips formed the phrases silently before speaking the last aloud.

Explosion at Governors' Summit. Lord Torrowin unharmed. Young Lord Mysric transported to Wylsaere for surgery.

"Prosthetist also en route…" I lowered the memorandum from my eyes, my heart sinking with it.

"This is your legacy." I couldn't keep

myself from jumping at the sudden break in the quietness.

No door had betrayed her with a labored groan. No light had spilled in from the hallway and saturated the floor with gold and shadow.

She'd always been there — and had merely chosen this moment to announce her presence.

"The courier came this morning. Xeanora has yet to know." Paia's face emerged from the blackness, sallow and near emotionless in what was left of the moonlight I'd summoned. She sat upright in a chair on the far side of the room as she stared in my direction. But her eyes never sought or met mine.

"I'm sorry." It seemed pointless — childish, even — apologizing.

"This is what you left behind." She responded, continuing. "The Torrowins are the only governing family without a claim reinforced by their ancestor's Legacy. We don't have Rathon to defend us from monsters. We have Rathon to guard us from the people who don't believe we should be in power."

"But I'm here now." I started, leaning forward as I shoved the sheets aside to free my legs and rose to my feet. But the workings of my mind were still in a deluge, and dark spots stole fragments of my sight. "I can show them who I am. I exist."

"And how would that help us?" She snapped when our eyes finally met, and I found myself drowning in the boundless cold emanating from the ones that had only recently accompanied a smile. "We still can't protect ourselves. Norrie — and Mysric can't protect themselves." Her voice broke — gave itself to anger, then anguish, then anger again. And the surrounding air seemed to chill in its wake. I pieced the flashes of memory together, grasped at the recollection of a room with books instead of walls.

Apples and toffee.

"Did you poison me?" My stomach churned as I gave voice to my fear; and standing, she surrendered her words to the silence to lend thought to her response.

"Your mother did what she could for you." She gazed at me, solemn. "I'm only doing the same for mine." With nothing left to be said, she crossed the bedroom floor and quickened her pace when she caught sight of my eyes darting between her face and the door. I held my breath as I pushed against the nearest bedpost to launch myself forward; but my legs couldn't carry me far enough, and I screamed in frustration as she pulled the door closed behind her.

"No!" I pounded the wood with open hands until I was sure my fingers would burst. "You don't know what you're doing!" I shouted to her, and the click of a key turning in a lock resonated through my insides as I slumped to my knees against the door.

"Maybe not." Her answer was barely audible from the other side. "But I'm willing to take that risk." I listened for a moment—for anything other than the silence that followed her words. But that was all it was, and I shrieked into the darkness again as I wrapped my arms around myself and crumpled onto the floor.

"Elynea?" I lifted my head from the ground, peeled my cheek from the intricate arrangement of tiles that no doubt left an impression on my skin, and slowly opened my eyes at my name.

I had no sense of time—no way to tell how much had passed. No moonlight breached the curtains drawn over the windows, and I suspected there would be no more calling any forth. I was confined to blindness once more. And waiting.

For whichever death suited Paia's purposes.

"Elynea?" It came again, in a slightly clearer whisper than the last.

I'd grown accustomed to the quiet—to the sound of my own shallow breaths as they poured from my mouth and onto the mosaic of blue, silver, and black. The edges were undefined, melting together in a disorienting kaleidoscope; and simply lying still felt like sinking into water. But slipping was easy. And I let each tide wash over me as I forfeited my body to the crawling oblivion and laid my head back down to rest on the floor.

"Elynea?" It was louder this time, and I was no longer certain that it was only occurring in my mind. "Elynea, it's me—Xeanora."

"Norrie?" I scrambled onto my knees to reach out my hand and press my fingertips against the door. "Norrie, you have to let me out."

"I—I can't unlock it without the key." She called to me, stuttering in a hushed voice. "But maybe you can."

"What do you mean?" I knit my eyebrows together at her suggestion, but I listened.

"You're one of the Morkoa." She said. "You can do anything." It was a sobering thought—one I'd just barely begun to understand. But her belief was all I needed. "Use the moonlight." I glanced over my shoulder at the darkened windows.

"The moon only ever shines in the darkness..." I murmured my mother's words to myself and stole another look to align both of the hands that I raised outstretched to face the window and the place where the two doors met. "I don't think this is what she had in mind." I grimaced, focusing on my palms and nothing else.

This wouldn't be like levitating droplets

of water or creating light.

I searched for the moon in the black field of night, let my consciousness roam the dreamlike world outside; and when I found it, a feeling I couldn't master took hold of me. It was overwhelming—like being caught in the waters of a distant memory.

Drowning in a deeper part of myself.

I shuddered at the hands of a sudden rush of cool air as the window bent inward and cracked, the iron frame wailing its death knell as it gave way with a crash. "Step back!" I warned. Glass and metal exploded across the floor. Glimmering shards sizzled over my head in a shower of apparent stars. And a bolt of moonlight burst through the tattered remnants of the drapes and into my body. It threaded itself through the conduit I'd improvised with my arms, and I gritted my teeth as I struggled to direct it by my will alone. I buried my face in my chest as a blinding light left my fingers to bore into the wood like a flaming sword—and shut my eyes as it dispelled the darkness entirely. And as day returned to night, I lifted my head from its refuge behind my arm and stared at the wreckage of splintered wood and broken glass.

The doors had been blown open, handles and hinges all but completely torn from place. What little remained of them still swayed back and forth, unable to abandon their purpose even with their life at an end. The carnage extended into the hall like the ruins of a cyclone, but Norrie was nowhere to be seen.

"Norrie?" The notion of digging for her body crushed beneath the rubble made me nauseous, and I strained to cast the thought aside. "I didn't kill her." I repeated the words in my head a thousand times in the hope that it would be true. "I didn't kill her."

But what if I had? No one could have survived it. Not if they were in the way.

My heart settled when two hazel eyes peeked out from the corridor, and Xeanora held out her hands to steady herself as she stepped through the debris strewn around her feet. Her bobble accelerated into a run when she caught sight of me; and before I could stand, she threw her arms around my neck.

"I'm so sorry." She squeezed me tighter. "I didn't know she would hurt you."

"It's okay." I breathed in reassurance as she let go, but she sat and gazed at me silently before reaching out a hand just inches from my face.

"Hold still." Norrie instructed when I flinched, and I held my breath as I obliged. She narrowed her eyes intently and moved her hand in a circular motion, as if she were swirling her fingers in a pool of water; and something rose inside me with the rhythm of her movements to follow her hand like a wave bowing to the pull of the moon. My heartbeat slowed in my chest, the extent of what she could possibly do occurring to me far too late for me to stop her.

But my trust wasn't misplaced.

She was drawing something out—I could feel it beading on my skin and running down my cheeks. And as the poison siphoned from my bloodstream and leaked out through my pores, the clouds that cluttered my tired mind began to clear. "That should do it."

"Where did you learn how to do that?" I asked when she lowered her hand into her lap; and she shrugged, nonchalant.

"School."

"Oh." I couldn't help but let my thoughts wander to what other lessons I'd missed.

"Almost everyone from Rynmmor eventually goes to Renasmere in Wenn's Reach." She went on as she helped me stagger to my feet. "Except the Wonders." She added. "They go to the Fallaore Academy."

"Are you…" I paused when I realized I'd already forgotten the word. "…one of those?"

"Mama thinks so." She replied; and I recalled Paia's reasoning for her name—talk of a patron goddess and three treasured gifts.

"Speaking of…" I allowed my voice to trail away as I looked over her head and out into the hall, knowing it wouldn't be too long before Lady Torrowin reappeared.

"You have to go." I didn't have to finish for her to understand.

"She's right." The hair on the nape of my neck bristled at the sound of another voice, and I cast my arm ahead of Norrie to dissuade its owner from coming any closer.

As if—somehow—the testament to my power dashed across the floor in pieces wasn't enough.

But the young man from Jaza remained in what was left of the doorway.

"No need, milady. I know who you are." Slowly, I lowered my hand.

"You won't stop us?" He shook his head at my question.

"I pledged my life to the House of Torrowin." He paused and bowed his head slightly in reverence, and I could only stare in response. "I will not break that vow. But you must go now—before Lady Torrowin realizes what you've done." He said, turning his head to inspect both sides of the hallway, and stepped backwards to allow us passage. Norrie tilted her eyes upward to find me and frowned—and hardened the expression on her face with renewed determination.

"Follow me." Clutching my hand in hers, she bounded over the heaps of timber and twisted iron and landed on her toes on the nearest tiles free of any debris; and I stumbled, less successfully, in pursuit of her. "We need to get to the pool. That's the closest way out." The silver-embroidered sash of her midnight blue robe flew behind her as she wrenched me forward and farther down the corridor.

"But I still don't know how to travel through the water." I responded, breathless. We were sprinting through the dark—dashing blindly toward what lay at the end of the hallway. The walls blurred past us. My naked feet slapped against the floor. And the iridescent sheen of moonlight captured within the pearl backing of the reflecting pool sparkled into view. But as we drew closer, the sound of flesh meeting stone began to soften—until the ground sucked at my skin and my steps were no longer sure; and I glanced down to investigate the cause.

Water—washing over the floor like an ocean tide. It flooded past my toes, creeping steadily as if I'd called it into being myself.

But I knew better.

The image of my startled face rippled beneath me as it rose and lashed at my legs, but it only spurred me onward at a faster pace.

I couldn't outrun it. I knew that. But if I reached the pool, it wouldn't matter. If I reached it—

"Mama, no!" My thoughts were interrupted by a scream as my feet were whipped up and out from under me and I was thrown roughly onto my back, and any oxygen dwelling in my lungs left my chest to burn in its absence. And as I lay gasping in the shallow water, I glimpsed her visage in the surface.

"Stay back, Xeanora!" The woman commanded, and the cacophony of splashing water and shouting fell away into bitter silence. "I think it's time you joined your brothers and sisters, Elynea." She spoke, flecks of water spraying over my forehead as she approached me from behind. It sloshed at my ears, snatched at my nostrils; and heaving, I floundered to my hands and knees in time to meet her shoes with my eyes. "The Morkoa are gone." A glint of silver cut the darkness in two, and I didn't have to look up to know what she was gripping in her hand. "Xaijena has no use for heroes anymore." I shivered — not at the thought of dying — no.

But what it meant to die here. Where my parents' blood once soaked the floors and screams echoed in the walls — all given for my life.

And I'd wasted it.

"I wasn't born to be a sacrifice." I whispered, my voice rising with the water around me. I raised my head to lock eyes with her and found her countenance marred by the droplets of water suspended between us. They were waiting, menacingly still in the quiet.

But they were mine.

I stood as she screeched and the blade came down, slicing the atmosphere and gathering dew as the spheres of water in its way burst into nothingness.

But it would pierce nothing else.

I caught her wrist in my fingers, digging my nails into her skin until rivulets of blood arced down the edges to mingle with the water below.

"*I* am Morkoa. And you will not treat me this way." The dagger slipped from her hand to fall at my feet and cast the water it displaced onto the skirt that clung to my ankles, and I kicked at the pommel with my heel to send it spinning to the opposite end of the corridor. I stole a step backward at Paia's sudden movement, only to watch her crumble to her knees and sob into her hands.

And for a moment, I imagined my mother falling into the same position in Cedar Crest when she realized I wouldn't be coming home.

"Ely?" I whirled to gaze at the pool bathed in silver light—and the girl two hundred and six years my junior waiting beside it.

"You know she was just trying to protect you—right?" I needed to be sure.

But she nodded, wordless, in answer. I left Paia's weeping form in the hallway to stand with her beneath the chandelier and peer into the water's depths, and she seemed to understand what I was thinking.

"You have to imagine what you want the most," she said, "and see yourself with it."

What I wanted most—I knew what that was.

I inched forward and closer to the edge, picturing Heather's smiling face as we laughed with Connor under our favorite tree; but two small arms wrapped themselves around my waist before I broke the mirror-like surface, and I turned to reciprocate her tight embrace with an encompassing hug of my own.

"I knew you weren't lost." She whispered into my chest, and when she let go, I knelt down to Norrie's level to set my hands on her shoulders.

"And I never will be." I promised and glanced at the woman behind her. "I'll come back when I can."

"Really?" She started. "What about—"

"Nothing is going to keep me from my family again." I held her in my arms once more; but this time, tearing away left me with hands much emptier than they'd been before. And with a sigh, I returned my attention to the reflecting pool. "Heather…" I murmured as I closed my eyes.

And I leapt into the unknown.

Chapter Seventeen

Ye Who Enter Here

$\mathcal{I}$ gasped for air as I burst out of the water and reached out for something to grab onto, ripping a handful of grass up from the ground. Grasping desperately, I crawled onto the grass and fought to catch my breath. It was warm, but the cold that had nearly claimed me in Cedar Crest still clung to my skin...and the clothes that seemed to be perpetually sodden. I closed my eyes in the silence and let the moonlight fall onto my back and seep into my veins, and I felt the weight suddenly disappear as droplets of water bled from my gown and drifted away. I raised my head, and a sparkling landscape of willow trees and rosebushes filled my eyes. There were marble fountains—as many as half a dozen— scattered across the garden and laden in golden lights. I rose to my feet, afraid that I had found myself in another chamber of the cemetery; but a gentle breeze swirled through my hair and into the branches of the nearest willow standing behind me, and I knew that I was outside.

"Where?" I said aloud—if only to myself—and stepped towards the nearest fountain, realizing that the lights weren't lights at all. I narrowed my eyes as the tiny silhouette of a boy sharpened in the midst of the glow that surrounded him.

"Nunnehi…" It was a whisper—faint like the whistle of the wind. I turned at the sound of it, my eyes searching for the source of the voice.

"Who's there?" My words echoed in the darkness. Nothing. It was quiet…just as it had been before. "Come out!" I commanded the silence, as if I expected it to obey. "Come out, or I swear, I'll—" There was a rustling in the bushes on the other side of the garden, and I stared at them in apprehension. I winced when the palms of my hands began to burn furiously, and I looked down at them to find the cause of it. Two blinding bright lights burst out of them— almost as if I were holding the stars in my fingers.

"My apologies…" A pair of amber eyes emerged from the shadows. "I thought you were another one." They darted to my glowing hands and then back to my face; and with a whimper, the figure retreated into the trees.

"No, wait!" I called out to it, shaking my

hands in an attempt to chase the light away. "I'm not going to hurt you." I insisted, adding, "I probably couldn't if I tried." I held out my palms when they were no longer shining. "Look, see? I have no idea what I'm doing." I joked, and the outline of a young woman reluctantly revealed itself. My eyes widened as I stared at her, speechless. She stood before me like a faded picture, bereft of color and dressed in clothes reminiscent of a time before my own. I could see the tree branches directly behind her as she stepped towards me, and I blinked to reassure myself of what I was seeing. "Are you—"

"A ghost? I—I don't think so." She glanced at her own transparent fingers, stuttering. "It's been so long, I can't remember." The long black hair that appeared to have been pulled into a bun long ago now fell unkempt over her face; and when she wrapped her arms around herself, I caught a glimpse of a dull jagged 'L' scarring her skin.

"What year was it…when he brought you here?" I asked her; and at once, she lowered her sullen face.

"The thirty-eighth year of the nineteenth century…" My heart stopped in my chest at those words. She had been here almost as long as I'd been gone. "I—I stopped counting the years after a while."

Wait.

"Were you there during the Trail of

Tears?" I knew the year sounded familiar. She wrinkled her forehead, frowning.

"Was that what they called it?" She paused. "It fits. All I remember is feeling cold. We started walking the month of the Long Night's Moon. We were meant to take a ferry across a river, but there was something else." She strained to pluck it from her memory. "There were—there were two full moons. I thought it strange but nothing more—not until the night of the second of them. I fell asleep under Mantle Rock and awoke in a much darker place." Her voice trembled with a fear I'd only seen in Adrienne's eyes. "And this," she gestured to her ghoulish appearance, "this is what happens to people like us when we stay too long. I suppose it's a gift: I won't have to exist for much longer." I looked at her sadly.

A century and a half.

"There are other girls here, right?" She didn't answer. "You said you thought I was another one. Can you take me to the rest?" I pleaded with her; and she stared at me, her eyes wide.

"Are you insane?" She asked, incredulous. "Surely, you'll be trapped here, too. There's no way out."

"You know that's not true." I insisted; and for a moment, the color seemed to return to her face.

"She made it?" I nodded, and her eyes

started to fill with tears.

"You can get out, too—*all* of you. That's why I'm here." I explained. "I just need to know where they are." She hesitated at my words but eventually reached out her spectral hand, glancing behind her back as if she expected someone to be waiting there. I took hold of her fingers and was surprised to find that they were just as solid as mine.

"Come with me." She tightened her grip and pulled me around the bushes and into the trees that had served as her hiding place. I watched as she bent down to brush away a handful of leaves from the ground, revealing the intricate design of an iron grate; and she stood, stealing a step back as she spoke. "This will lead you to them." I pulled the grate up from the cobblestone pavement and set it aside; and it scraped against the stone surface in the quiet.

"Thank you." I breathed and bit my lip as I looked into the darkness that awaited me.

"I'm coming with you." I gazed up at her in surprise, but she didn't falter. "You don't know what's on the other side."

"Are you sure?" I asked her, and she nodded in response. "All right." I sighed. "Just stay behind me." Slowly, I lowered myself into the opening in the ground and let my legs dangle freely when I found a seat on the edge. I narrowed my eyes in an attempt to peer into the depths below, but it was too dark to see past my feet. "It's not too far down?" I turned as I asked her, and she shook her head. Without another thought, I slid off the side and landed on my feet in the shadows. A cloud of dust rose up from the ground and entangled itself in my hair, and I lifted my head toward the ceiling as the girl with the amber eyes dropped down beside me. "I don't think I caught your name." I mentioned, and she stood.

"Charlotte." She started. "Charlotte Blackwolf."

"Melissa Moonwater." I answered before returning my attention to the tunnel that stretched on before us.

I couldn't help but wonder what awaited me at the end of it, but something in me made me glad that I wasn't alone.

"I'm afraid it's too dark." I heard Charlotte remark behind me. I glanced down at my hands and peered at the calloused skin of my palms expectantly.

"Not for long." I muttered to myself as two rays of light flickered in the darkness, and I held my hands out in front of me to illuminate the way. Like the stone arches that I had seen when I had first set foot in Rynmoor, red bricks arced themselves over our heads and kept the walls of rocks and clay from caving in on us.

"A useful gift." She commented as I led the way into the unknown, and I stole a glimpse at her from over my shoulder.

"It's a long story." I replied.

It'd only been a month, and so much had changed.

"You don't seem so surprised." I remarked, gazing at the ground as a muddy brown mouse scurried past my feet.

They all looked the same, whether they were finding shelter in my parents' stables or somewhere much farther away.

"I suppose after spending as long as I have here, I've learned that nothing is impossible." She responded, somber. "I've seen enough monsters to last me a lifetime."

I'm sure she had.

I lowered my hands in disappointment when the path suddenly came to an end, and Charlotte nearly collided with me before she realized that I had stopped.

"What's the mat−" She paused when she saw the brick wall standing silently in front of us, shaking her head. "No. That wasn't there before."

"Are you sure?" I frowned, disheartened.

Everything I had fought for was only a few steps away; and now, I couldn't reach it.

"Absolutely." She insisted. "I was just here." For a moment, I merely stared at it as I felt my heart sink into my stomach and then back to the girl slowly fading away beside me.

"But−but it was dark…You couldn't have seen it." I stuttered, and she raised her eyebrows at my words.

"I don't understand." I stole a step forward and set my hand on the wall, tracing the cracks of the weathered bricks with my fingers.

"I think you went through it." I turned to face her, only to find her looking down at her arms.

"I suppose that's possible…" She murmured to herself and raised her head to set her eyes on me. "I thought I had more time."

"I'm saving you, too." I reminded her; and she nodded, but nothing I could say would take that look out of her eyes. "Do you think you can help me get through?"

"I—I think so." Hesitantly, she joined me at the wall and swallowed, just as terrified as I was. But she reached out her hand, immediately jumping back in surprise when her fingertips disappeared. "Are you ready?" She asked me, and I grasped her hand in response. Closing my eyes, I let her pull me to the other side; and suddenly, the warmth that I had felt before was gone. The fresh summer air had given way to an atmosphere that tasted stale and bitter in my mouth and smelled of mold and rotting wood. The eerie silence was only broken by the constant dripping of water, faint like a whisper—but loud enough to haunt me. A soft whimper drifted up to my ears from the floor; and I lifted my right hand over my head, dissolving the darkness. At once, a chorus of weakened screams and clinking metal erupted in the newly found light; and I lowered it. The moonlight cast shadowy pillars on the furthest wall as it moved from the ceiling to the ground, and the silhouettes of thin arms and legs came into view.

"Heather? Heather, I'm here." I fell to my hands and knees at the foot of the nearest crate and peered inside, only to find that it was empty.

"Melissa Moonwater?" The air began to ripple around the disembodied voice, and what little light that entered through the slits in the crate shifted until a small mass formed inside. And it lifted its head to reveal a face that I hadn't seen in a long time. She scrambled from the back of the wooden box to see me more clearly. "What are you doing? How did you escape?"

"I didn't." Iliana's deep brown eyes widened as I spoke.

"Then why would you come here?" Her voice trembled in her throat. "You shouldn't have come." She shrank back, the gravity of the situation clear in those frightened eyes.

"I'm here to help." I insisted and glanced back at Charlotte before placing my hand on the latch, and it was instantly reduced to nothing. Swinging open the door, I crawled inside and held out my hand for her to take it. But she only gazed at it, stunned.

"I never thought I'd see anything like

that." She marveled as she grasped it, shaking nervously as she struggled out of the crate and into the open. Straw clung to her hair and clothes, and the scars that riddled Adrienne's and Charlotte's arms appeared just as horrifying on hers.

"Charlotte," I turned to the girl with the wolf-like eyes, "stay with Iliana. I'm going to help everyone else." I told her, and she nodded her head at my request. I rose to my feet; and suddenly, a loud creak split the darkness in two—the immediate onset of fear extinguishing my torch of moonlight. Before I could catch my breath, Iliana shoved me inside the mouth of her prison and forced herself to join me. "What's going on?" I whispered, disoriented as she placed her hand on me.

A strange feeling came over me, like the kind of seasick I'd wished I'd experienced all my life—if only to know what being on the ocean was like.

And I stared at my arms as they at once ceased to exist…or ceased to be seen.

"*Infierno…*" She murmured under her breath, horrified.

"No. No…no. Please, no more." That voice. I could never forget that voice.

I flinched when the quiet gave way to a bloodcurdling scream; and all I could do was listen as it continued, leaning against Iliana in an effort to keep myself from making any noise. It stopped for a moment—only a moment—and started again, more desperate than the first. It shook my insides, twisted my stomach into an unrecognizable mess of knots. I wanted to cover my ears for as long as I could—shut my eyes until it ended. But the screams wouldn't stop, and my eyes filled with tears when I realized that I couldn't do anything.

Only wait. Like I had no power at all.

I lifted my head up from Iliana's shoulder when a sickening silence fell over the room, and the same creak that had frightened so many sent relief flooding into the darkness. I crawled to the other side of the box, to the voice that I had heard; and I peered through the slits and into the next crate. There, trembling on the hay-covered floor, was the pale skin and wispy red hair that I had missed so much.

"Heather?" I called her name, but she didn't move. "Heather." I said it again. Slowly, she raised her head; and her green eyes lit up at the sight of me.

"Melissa?" She gazed at me, at first confused.

"Yeah." I nodded, and she burst into tears when she understood.

"You didn't stop?" I shook my head in response and fit my fingers through the opening; and she did the same, our hands grasping at each other until I found her and squeezed her tightly.

"I'm going to get you out." I promised. I
scrambled out of the wooden crate as quickly as
I could and raced to the neighboring box to rip
the planks of wood away from the door with my
own strength and adrenaline, not even bothering
to call up a burst of moonlight to blast it open.
And as if she always had been, Heather was in
my arms. She was wearing what I had last seen
her in: the gray plaid short-sleeved shirt and
dark blue jeans, her powder blue winter coat
tied around her waist. Her jagged scars had been
torn open; and blood ran down her elbows in
crimson lines as she embraced me, sobbing. "We
have to get out of here," I looked to Charlotte
and Iliana, "before he comes back."

"No, Melissa, you—you don't
understand." Heather stuttered as she tried to
explain, and I turned my head to face her again.

"What don't I understand?" I asked her;
and she stared at me, unblinking.

"There are two of them." And then I
knew.

Adrienne had only seen one face.

Chapter Eighteen
Born of Blood

$\mathcal{I}$ flew into a frenzy, holding my hand up to the locks to disintegrate them and throwing the doors open. Much frailer versions of Rebecca, Willow, Valerie, and Jasmine emerged from the darkness that had held them, looking more like ghosts than the girls that I had remembered; and they helped each other stand before rushing to the aid of two girls with faces I couldn't recognize. But the hair — April Lawson had that same red hair, only twisted in a braid that fell past her shoulders. She stood terrified in a polka dot swimsuit alongside a raven-haired girl that I could only guess was Chelsea Banneker. I watched as Heather held out a bloodstained hand at the mouth of an open crate, and Stephanie slowly crawled out of the shadows. The both of them rose to their feet, but Heather's eyes suddenly widened as if she sensed something in the air. At first, I thought it was the moonlight that I held in my hand; but when I lifted my palm to my narrowing eyes, I knew that it couldn't be.

It was already happening.

She had begun to flicker in and out of sight like a broken light. She looked up from her trembling fingers when she caught a glimpse of my reaction.

"It's okay. It'll go away. It always does." She reassured me, not sounding very sure herself. I glanced at Charlotte, and she gazed at me with the same solemnity that she had before.

"Do you think you can get us through that wall?" I asked her. Without a word, she nodded; and I pointed the others in the direction of the moldering brick wall.

"How are we going to get past that?" Eva wondered aloud, incredulous.

"This world changes you—if you're here long enough." Charlotte answered her, already only a foot from the wall, and placed her hand on the stones; and she closed her eyes as her shoulders rose with a labored breath. But her eyelids flew open immediately, and she looked down at her hand as she pushed it against the wall.

Nothing. Nothing at all.

"I don't understand. I don't—it worked before..."

"Charlotte?" I called her name, but she didn't answer. She remained at the wall, quiet as she leaned her head against it.

"No...no...no!" Her murmured words grew into a scream of frustration, and she struck the bricks with a clenched fist. And she turned to me, her amber eyes filling with tears. "I can't do it..." Her hand fell to her side, and blood trickled from her knuckles and onto the floor.

"We're all going to die here, aren't we?" Stephanie whispered.

As much as I hated it, I couldn't help but think the same thing.

"No." I shook my head and rushed past her, past the wooden crates and towards the mysterious door looming on the other side of the room. "We're not."

"Melissa, no!" Heather shouted just before I reached out my hand to set it on the handle. "We'd be going straight to them."

"I came here to take you home, and that's what I'm going to do." I replied, gazing out at all of them as I spoke. She still stared at me in terror, but I placed my fingers on the handle once again. And I pulled the door open. The darkness that I had expected was absent on the other side, a warm yellow light spilling into the room instead. It accosted my eyes and riddled my sight with spots; and I realized, for a moment, that I had forgotten how the sunshine felt on my skin.

But it felt so much like it—whatever it was.

I looked over my shoulder and at the others and beckoned for them to follow me. But they didn't.

"Come on." I lowered my voice when the thought of being heard by someone else occurred to me. "What are you waiting for?"

"What if it's worse?" Jennifer said, with a fear that I knew I couldn't comprehend. And still, I gestured to the open doorway.

"A few of us can go and search for a way out, then I'll send someone back to lead the way." The air suddenly shifted at my words as Heather stepped forward.

"I'll go." She volunteered as Charlotte and Iliana joined her side; and the three of them left the other eleven in the darkness to stand with me at the door. I moved aside to let them through the doorway before me and paused to look back at them one last time.

"We'll be back." I promised. And the door closed behind me.

"Wow." Iliana was the first to speak in the newly found quietness, and I turned around to see her staring up at the ceiling.

And immediately, I was standing in front of Adrienne's door on that first December night.

Golden branches twisted in and out of themselves over panes of frosted glass, lights that I could only guess were the constellations dancing beyond them. The immense skylight ended where two oak walls began, and the dark wood glowed amber in the nearly blinding light from above.

"Where are we?"

"Rynmoor." I whispered to myself.

There was still so much I hadn't seen—a world I hadn't yet come to know.

"Rin-more?" Charlotte repeated, crinkling her forehead.

"This is where I was born." I answered her as I started down the hall; and Heather hurried after me, keeping close to the eastern wall.

"What are you talking about?" She caught up with me. "You've lived in Cedar Crest your whole life." She told me, so confident in what she knew; but I shook my head.

Not my *whole* life.

"It's a long story…" I murmured.

I couldn't imagine her believing me—not at first.

Charlotte appeared on my other side, speaking quietly.

"When I saw you, I assumed…" Her voice trailed away. "You *are* Cherokee?"

"My parents are." I answered, hoping that she wouldn't need an explanation. She peered at me in curiosity but continued.

"Then your mother and father told you the story of the Hunter and the Corn Woman?"

She wanted to know, inquiring earnestly; but I shook my head, and she sighed in disappointment. "In the beginning, Kana'ti the Hunter and his wife Selu the Corn Woman had one child, a boy that they loved dearly. But one day, while the boy was playing by the river, another boy sprang up from the blood of the animals that Kana'ti had killed; and Kana'ti and Selu took him home as their own and tamed him...But he was born from blood."

"What does that mean?" I asked, terrified of what her answer would be. She leaned forward, the horror clear on her face.

"Nothing born from blood can be good." She said. "No child of death can be tamed. The two sons grew to be called the Twin Thunder Boys, but the wild brother never abandoned his parentage. His influence on the other became much greater than Kana'ti could handle. When the two of them witnessed Selu using magic to make corn, they murdered her and mounted her head on the roof. And at her final request, they dragged her body around the house to ensure that corn would grow wherever her blood touched the ground."

"No." I shook my head. "That can't be it." I tried to convince myself; but the more I thought of it, the more I knew it to be true. "If the Twin Thunder Boys are his sons..." I stopped.

One face.

"It wasn't him..." I whispered; and suddenly, I found Iliana beside me.

"So what you did back there—what's happening to us is different?" She frowned when I nodded.

"It's like...you're turning into ghosts." I tried to explain it. "You've all been here so long." But how it was affecting them: the invisibility, the flickering—I couldn't begin to understand it myself. Heather looked down at the floor for a moment as she walked a few steps behind me.

"I go somewhere when I disappear." She confessed, and I paused to listen. "At first, I thought it was a dream; but after a while, I realized that it wasn't." She continued, gazing up at me. "I saw Matthew there, once. Did he come here looking for me, too?" I stared at her as my throat began to hurt, swallowing hard in an attempt to make it go away. But it wouldn't. And my eyes burned when I opened my mouth, seeing him again that night as he trembled in the crimson snow.

"Wait..." Iliana interjected; and in the blink of an eye, she was gone. My blood ran cold when I finally heard it, and I yearned for the silence that had seemed so terrifying before.

Footsteps. They grew louder, my heart quickening in my chest as a shadow passed just around the corner; and as I glanced behind and beyond me, I realized that there was no escape. I stood there in the middle of the hallway as I bit my lip—so hard, I tore the skin and tasted blood. And I waited for whatever was coming. My knuckles whitened when I shakily curled my hands into fists; and I quickly looked down as two spheres of light formed inside them, something growing inside me that I hadn't quite discovered yet.

"Stay back!" I warned, holding out my hands in a threat for the stranger to keep its distance. I held my breath as the shadow moved across the floor, but it was only connected to one pair of feet.

Deerskin trousers—and a quiver strapped against his bare back and between his broad shoulders…The Hunter.

I blinked as he advanced towards me slowly, his hands over his head. He looked so different—like something I'd never seen before. His face was the same; but the light clung to his skin like it was a part of him, erasing the scars and leaving perfection in their place.

"Caleb…" I caught myself. Caleb didn't exist. "Kana'ti…"

"Elynea…" It sounded so foreign in his voice—I'd always been Moongirl; but it felt just as familiar—like I'd been waiting for him to say it my whole life.

No.

I chased the thought away. The curse— that's all it was.

I retreated when he took another step forward. "I'm not going to hurt you," his eyes darted to Heather and Charlotte, "any of you." The air thickened behind me as Iliana slowly revealed herself, and he nodded in her direction. "That's new."

"I believe you."

"Huh," he chuckled a little, "'remind you of somethin'?" He smiled—oh, that smile. However much had changed, he sent me back to the stables; and my heart hurt for how innocent I had been then. How oblivious. But I came to my senses, lowering my hands and extinguishing the light that burned within them.

"How did you find me?" I wanted an answer.

"This is my home. You came to me." He replied, as perplexed as I was. "I—I don't understand." He shook his head. "Why did you come here?" For a moment, I simply stared at him, searching for the truth.

"You don't know…" I looked to Charlotte for an explanation, but she shook her head sadly. How couldn't he?

"Know what?" He asked, and I saw something in his eyes—the child that I never knew existed.

"Your sons—they took my friends." His eyes widened at my words.

"No." He wouldn't believe it. "They—they wouldn't." Charlotte took a step forward.

"I've been here for two hundred years." She told him. "They kept telling me that I wasn't good enough—that I had to try." His eyes fell to the floor when she pulled back her sleeves to show him the scars.

"I think they thought that if they found me, then I could replace her." I gazed down at my fingers as I spoke, moving towards him. "Kana'ti," he lifted his head when I called his name, his brown eyes wide, "what do you remember from that night?"

"Um," he scratched his head as he fought to recall it, "I'd just come back from hunting, and Selu—Selu had insisted that we take a walk in the woods. But when I returned home, I couldn't find her. And then, I saw the blood." His eyes glossed over with tears, and he stared at the floor once again. "It led to a field of corn— it was so thick. I didn't know how it got there. At first, I didn't see the body. But when I found her, her head—her head wasn't with it." He stuttered; and he took a deep breath to calm himself, shaking. "My sons—they'd been sitting just outside the field, and I told them to go inside. That's when," he cleared his throat, "that's when I saw that her head was…on the roof. She needed to be whole—the way I remembered her. So I brought her down and held her in my arms." He wept, brushing the tears off of his face. "Why are you asking me this?"

"They killed her." I breathed.

"What?" He looked up at me in confusion.

"They saw what she could do, and they killed her for it." I explained, and he placed his hand on his forehead.

"N—no. They're children. They couldn't…" His voice trailed away as I continued.

"Before she died, she told them to drag her body around the house so corn would still grow even after she was gone." My words gave him pause, causing him to meet my eyes with a gaze of disbelief.

"How could you know that?"

"Melissa…" Heather set her hand on my shoulder in an attempt to hold me back, but I glanced back at her from over my shoulder as I drew closer anyway.

"It's okay." I whispered and turned to face him. "The world where you found me— they tell stories about you. But they don't all know that you're real. They don't know that any of this is real. I know that you've been searching for me; but your sons have been, too, and not in the way that you would have wanted." I grasped his hands, squeezing them tightly. "My friends don't belong here. Kana'ti," I called his name to claim his attention, "you have to help us." He clasped his fingers around mine in return, speaking loud enough for the others to hear.

"There's a path through the foyer that will bring you to the terrace." He began and looked to Charlotte, Heather, and Iliana earnestly. "I'll lead you to it."

"Are we close?" I asked as I trailed him through the palace halls, meandering around corners and past walls that captured out shadows and threw them against the wooden panels.

"Almost." He stopped abruptly as we came upon a spacious room and gestured to the towering double doors on the opposite side. "That's the terrace." I turned to Iliana.

"I'll get the others." She said and disappeared before my eyes.

"Okay." I sighed, finally able to breathe. I let myself take in my surroundings for a moment, my eyes darting from the grand staircase behind us to the two armchairs encumbered with chocolate brown furs. The first was fairly worn, but the other—it looked like it hadn't been touched for a very long time. I couldn't help but stare at it and imagine what she must have been like—and how he lived without seeing her still sitting in that chair, smiling and laughing like she always had before. I felt his hand on my shoulder and jumped, and I bit my lip when I realized how terrified I still was.

"How did you know?" I blinked, not entirely sure what he was asking. "Who I was?" He added.

"Orion and Moongirl..." I smiled a little. "You were telling me since the night I met you." He flashed me a grin of his own. "That and your acting. It's Cedar Crest—not Hick Town, USA." I added.

"Of course." He chuckled and glanced at the empty old chair, suddenly sullen; and I knew what he was seeing. "You know—" He began, but Heather's voice prevented him from finishing.

"What about *them*?" She turned to me. "They're still out there."

"I'll take care of it—once you're all home." He promised her, and her eyes fell on my face before settling once again on his.

"How far is that?" Her question silenced me, and I looked to Kana'ti for a reasonable explanation. But he stared back at me with the same bewilderment. "We're not in Oklahoma, are we?" The both of us opened our mouths in an effort to respond, but Heather lifted her head to gaze up at the ceiling at once; and I witnessed the light on her skin start to flicker.

"That's not you, is it?" I wasn't sure if I really wanted an answer. We locked eyes as she lowered her face.

"No. You?" I shook my head silently.

I didn't think my gift could have caused

something like that.

The sudden clap of feet meeting the floor echoed into the foyer, sending the four of us scrambling for each other. Heather let out a scream as one of the lamps mounted on the wall exploded in a shower of sizzling glass, and Kana'ti pulled me close to him as if his arms would keep me safe. Charlotte covered her head as she whispered, frantic.

"What is this?" At her words, Iliana came running out of the corridor, eleven other faces trailing close behind.

"What's going on?" She wanted to know, breathless. "The lights started going crazy once we got to the hall." I swallowed when I heard the Hunter's heart skip a beat in his chest.

"It's my sons..." His voice trailed away as he murmured. I froze as a thunderous boom erupted from above and quickly seeped down into the walls, shaking the floor and causing the two armchairs to wobble in place. I trembled where I stood when there was suddenly nothing but silence, and darkness consumed the light around me. It was quiet for what felt like minutes — save for the whimpering that found its way into my ears, and Kana'ti shouted into the void. "Enough!"

It was terrifying — how his voice seemed to match the thunder. For a moment, I had forgotten who he was.

A deafening crack split the blackness in

two when lightning struck the floorboards a few feet away from me, leaving smoldering ashes in its wake. And two pairs of glowing silver eyes met my own.

Chapter Nineteen
What We Find in Death

"Melissa..." Kana'ti whispered to me, standing motionless in the darkness.

"Yeah?" I couldn't even look at him. I was still trapped inside those menacing eyes.

"Now would be a good time to run." The blood was pounding in my ears so loudly, I could barely understand what he was saying.

"Not gonna happen." I answered him, and he sighed in exasperation. "Hey," I said when I finally turned my head to face him, "it's not over yet." Taking a deep breath, I stole a step forward. Tyler eyed me for a moment in silence, as if he were seeing someone else.

"Are you Lyn?" He gazed at me expectantly, eyes wide; and I couldn't come to terms with what he'd done.

"Yeah. That's me." I replied. His face lit up with a beaming smile at my response.

"I was hoping it was you." I returned it with one of my own for a split second, forgetting everything that I had learned. But it immediately fell away.

"You took our playthings..." Trenton crossed his arms as he pouted, glaring at the man standing beside me. "Give them back." But he shook his head.

"No." He started. "They're *people*, not objects." The little boy narrowed his eyes in an attempt to understand.

"But it's fun." Those words sent a chill down my spine, and I shivered in the sudden cold.

Was I imagining it? I wasn't sure of anything anymore.

"Tyler," I looked to him in desperation, "you're hurting people. I know you've been looking for me, and I'm here. So you can let them go." I told him; and once again, I was staring at a pair of innocent brown eyes. I grinned, kneeling to meet his level as he slowly inched towards me. "I know what happened to your mom," I began, "but it's okay. But trying to replace her like this is wrong." He faltered as I spoke and glanced at Trenton from over his shoulder. Wordlessly, they gazed at each other; and my heart sank into my stomach when he returned to his side.

"She was a witch." Trenton snapped in response. "Witches die." I turned, horrified, to Charlotte; and the expression on her face was enough.

"I understand." I said, and Kana'ti stared at me in surprise. "Witches can be scary, but your mother was never going to hurt you." I swallowed, gathering up the strength that I needed. "But you have to understand: I'm taking my friends home." I whirled to lead the girls to the door, but something grasped my hand and held me back.

Tyler.

"Please don't go." He pleaded with me, frowning. "Daddy needs you. Stay." I opened my mouth to speak, but the words failed me. And I looked back at Kana'ti, lingering a little longer than I should have.

He didn't have to say anything. I already knew it was true.

I mouthed the words "I'm sorry" and gazed at Tyler apologetically.

"I can't."

"You will." I turned in apprehension to find that Trenton's young face had hardened in anger, and his hand had suddenly been raised over his head. There was a whimper at once, and it slowly built into a muffled scream.

"Melissa!" Heather shouted my name, sending me in her direction—but only to find that she wasn't the one who had screamed. Rebecca and Willow shrieked as Valerie stumbled backward, covering her face with her hands as blood hemorrhaged out of her eyes and seeped through her fingers; and deep burgundy bruises flowered over her arms and legs.

"Make it stop!" She screeched again and again, but there was nothing I could do. "Make it stop!"

"What are you doing?!" I cried, widening my own eyes in terror.

"This is home now!" Trenton barked as he tightened his hand into a fist, and Valerie's screams only grew louder and much more horrifying. She clawed at her forehead as crimson streamed out of her eyes and nose and stained her skin; and I looked to Kana'ti, helpless.

"Stop this!" The room trembled under the weight of his voice; and I lifted my head to watch the chandelier sway a little above me, returning my attention to the Hunter and his children when I realized that he had seized Trenton's arm. "Let this end." He scolded him through clenched teeth. Trenton's eyes darted to his wrist and then back to his father's face in a silent glare. And then he spoke.

"I don't think I like you anymore." A great flash of blinding light consumed the foyer before I could cover my eyes, and it died as quickly as it had appeared.

"Kana'ti…" Sightless, I reached for him; and instantly, I felt his hands pull me towards him.

"I'm here." His golden aura chased the dark spots away from my sight, and I blinked to be sure of what I was seeing.

Tyler and Trenton were gone.

"Where did they go?" I breathed as I searched the room for a clue — anything that could have hinted to where they had disappeared to. A heavy sigh met my ears from behind me; and I whirled to find that the screaming had stopped, and Valerie's bruises began to recede into themselves.

"They're playing with us." Willow shuddered as she gingerly wrapped her arms around a weeping Valerie, and Gabrielle stepped forward.

"Melissa, you have to kill them."

"Whoa…" The thought hadn't even occurred to me. "Since when has that ever been okay?"

They were still children.

The rumbling of distant thunder froze my heart in my chest, and I turned my head in the direction that it was coming from.

The stairs.

"Everybody down!" I yelled just as the atmosphere rippled, and a bright streak of electric blue shot across the room from the landing. It crackled over Jasmine's head and struck a vase standing by the wall, sending shards of porcelain flying onto the floor.

Despite my reservations, they were definitely intent on killing me.

"Have you changed your mind, yet?" Jasmine called out over the bellowing thunder and earsplitting cacophony of lightning striking the walls and disintegrating everything in its path, and I hated myself for considering it.

"There has to be another way!" A powerful gale outmatched my words and sent my hair rushing violently around my head as I covered my ears. "There has to be another way…" I whispered to myself when something cold and wet started to fall on my back; and immediately, I was terrified that it was blood. But when I raised my face towards the ceiling, I knew that it wasn't.

Rain. It soaked the air in the form of a cloud of mist, growing heavier until large drops fell like bullets over my shoulders. And I was standing in a tempest in a single room.

I gazed at the broken table engulfed in flames dying in the pouring rain; and Heather lifted her head up from behind it, her light green eyes illuminated in the hellish glow.

"Heather!" I flailed my arm to gain her attention, holding my breath as she crawled through the rubble to reach me. Her auburn hair was plastered to the left side of her face with blood. "Are you okay?"

It sounded like a stupid question to ask.

But she nodded.

"Yeah. Yeah, I'm okay." I let out a sigh when she answered.

She wouldn't be.

"I think I know where you've been going." I breathed, and she leaned forward to hear more.

"Really?" She stuttered. "H—how?"

I can't tell her. How could I tell her?

I bit my lip.

"I need your help."

I slowly rose to my feet and stared up at the rafters, blinking my eyes to keep the rain from blinding me. I glanced over my shoulder at Heather standing behind me and gave her a nervous smile. And I returned my gaze to the landing.

"I'll stay." I spoke; and for what felt like minutes, I waited. But nothing happened. "Did you hear me?" I raised my voice. "I said I'll stay!"

"You won't leave?" I turned towards Tyler's voice to find the both of them waiting by their mother's chair, and I shook my head.

"No." Trenton's eyes suddenly softened at my answer; and Tyler sprinted to wrap his arms around me, beaming. "It's okay." I held my hand out for Trenton when he lowered his head to stare at the ground beneath him. And he smiled. He took my hand, and the world around us began to shift in and out of focus.

The grand staircase disappeared from my sight, only to reappear covered in thick vines that strangled the twin bannisters and gave birth to roses. A field of grass emerged from the tile floor and rose high above my ankles, and the warmth of the sun enveloped every part of me. The sun.

We were outside.

I squinted my eyes in the newfound light to see that the violent storm had gone and left only silence in its place. And I breathed a sigh of relief.

"Melissa!" A figure darted across the open field to meet me; and as it came into view, I realized that it was Heather. I glanced down at my hands, trembling.

They were empty. And I was alone.

"Melissa!" She panted as she raced through the tall grass, pushing the blades away from her waist; and I hurried to her, closing the space between us in a grateful hug.

"I don't know where they went…" I uttered when I released her. I scanned the great expanse for the silhouettes of two little boys, but there was nothing.

"There's an apple tree," Heather started; and I turned to listen, "by the river. I was hungry one night, and it was there when I fell asleep."

"And you didn't eat from it?" I asked her, sure that I would have.

I would have stayed here, too — or at least tried my hardest. It was so peaceful here. I would have done anything I could to stay in a place like this if I knew the Twins were my only other option.

She shook her head.

"No. I wanted to." She confessed. "But then I wondered what that would make me — while everyone else was starving. And then, it started getting closer…every time I came back — like it wanted me take one. That's where I left them."

"Oh…" I shuddered silently as I took in my surroundings.

Suddenly, even the sea of grass that we were standing in felt different — like the monsters lurking beneath it had come to life.

"It looked like home, before." Heather mentioned, lost in this new place. "It's never been like this."

"Maybe, it changes." I suggested — more to myself than anyone else. "Maybe, it's whatever you want it to be." She stared off into the distance, seeing nothing more than a field of grass: still and unending.

"What is 'it'?" She wanted to know. "And why was Matthew here?" I could hear my heart beating faster in the eerie silence.

"That's…that's what I've been meaning to tell you." My voice cracked when I spoke, and she gazed at me expectantly as I cleared my throat. "He — we went to look for you on the island. But something else was waiting for us there." I sputtered through my answer. "I didn't know — I didn't know what I do now. I didn't know what was out there."

"What are you saying?" She asked me. I breathed deeply to keep myself from falling apart, but it wasn't enough. And she looked at me with tearful eyes. "Melissa, what are you saying?"

"I — I think this is Death." I wasn't sure if saying it would make it better, but now I knew that it wouldn't. She covered her mouth as I watched her crumble from the inside, and she sank into the grass as she wept without a sound. I bent down in front of her, hating myself for something I couldn't possibly have stopped.

"Were you there?" It was a whisper, barely audible in the silence.

"Yeah." It was all I said.

"How did he —" I couldn't let her finish.

"That's not something —" I shook my head.

She didn't need to know. And then, I remembered.

"He wanted me to tell you something." She lifted her head up from her hands at my words. "He tried."

Heather and I stepped through the ruins of the foyer, through the puddles glowing in the light of the dying embers the Twin Thunder Boys had left behind. It was dark—I could barely make out the faces of Stephanie, Kerri, and April as they rose up from behind the overturned armchairs they had used for shelter. I held my hand over my head and let the light of the moon bathe the room in silver. And one by one, the rest emerged from their hiding places.

"We weren't sure if you were coming back…" April sheepishly stepped forward; and Heather wrinkled her forehead, as if in an attempt to recall where they had met.

"It's over?" Charlotte hurried to greet me from the bottom of the grand staircase, her transparent skin losing its color all too quickly. I nodded my head.

"It's over." And she closed her eyes with a thankful sigh. Eva, Gabrielle, Jennifer, Jasmine, Valerie, Rebecca, Willow, and Chelsea—for the first time in months, I saw them smile; and I could finally breathe.

But…where—

"Where's Iliana?" I walked past Charlotte to stand in the center of foyer, holding my hand towards the darkest parts of the room. But she wasn't in any of them.

"There!" Kana'ti shouted, pointing to a marble pedestal where the remnants of an urn lay scattered at its base. Scarlet drops splattered on the floor from what appeared to be nothing; but the outline of Iliana Lopez materialized as the pillar crashed to the floor and split in half, and she slumped onto the tiles beside it. Without a thought, I raced to her, my feet shattering the amber mirrors on the floor as I ran through the water. I knelt down beside her as she stared up at the ceiling, pale lips trembling.

"Sorry." She spoke through shallow breaths. "I screwed up your rescue." She grimaced and placed her hand over her stomach, but it wasn't enough to cover the gaping hole. And I saw that it was rimmed with the singed fabric of her blouse.

Lightning. It was the only explanation.

"I guess I won't be going home after all." A tear escaped the corner of her eye and left her face to lose itself in the water below.

"No." Rebecca clasped her hands around hers and squeezed them tightly. "You're going home. All of us are." But she lifted her eyes to stare at me pleadingly, holding back tears of her own. "Can you do anything?" Whatever hope in her voice died when I shook my head.

"I think I can…" I turned my head when I heard Heather speak, and I found her gazing down at Iliana from where she was standing.

The way that she was staring at her — and then I knew.

"You're not—" I rose to my feet, whispering.

She couldn't.

"She's gonna die." She tried to reason with me. "If *you* could do it, wouldn't you?"

I couldn't say that I wouldn't.

"Then it's settled." She took my silence for an answer, bending down to join the others around her.

"What are you going to do?" Eva asked her from where she was sitting. Heather glanced up at her before setting her attention on Iliana once again, and she gingerly set a hand on her shoulder.

"There's a place that I can take her." She breathed in response. "Time freezes; wounds stop bleeding. But she can't go there alone. Someone's going to have to stay with her until we figure out how to fix this."

"I'll go." Rebecca replied, almost instantly. "She's my friend. I'll keep her safe."

"Okay." Heather looked over her shoulder to smile at me as she began to flicker in and out of sight. "I'll see you on the other side." And she was gone.

"Kana'ti..." He stood up from the floor and sprinted to me when I called his name, his wet dark hair clinging to the back of his neck.

"Yeah?" He reached out to touch my arm

as he spoke, and it was exactly as I had remembered.

But this time, there was no mystery. This was the way that it was supposed to be.

"Wait here until Heather comes back. The rest of us will meet you at the bridge." He narrowed his eyes; and for a moment, I thought it was in reaction to my request. "What's wrong?"

"Who told you to be afraid of me?" At first, I didn't understand the question.

"My grandfather—he said my parents gave me away to keep me from you." I stuttered, now knowing that it couldn't be true.

It was the Twin Thunder Boys that they feared.

"Your grandfather..." He stared down at the floor, perplexed. "I was there. The Wendigo..." He whispered, losing himself in his thoughts. "Melissa, he didn't survive." My heart stopped in my chest.

I wondered how the old man could stand the cold.

Connor.

Chapter Twenty
A Grave Exchange

"Melissa! Wait!" Kana'ti shouted to me as I turned and bolted toward the terrace doors and threw them open, suddenly blinded by the sunlight that came pouring in. But I ignored him, dashing down the stone steps and past the marble pillars that lined the pathway and cast massive shadows on the ground. A towering gate of bronze waited for me at the end of the path, and I pushed it out of my way and darted out into the street. A horse-drawn carriage sped past me, carrying a gust of wind with it; and I stopped, frantically looking around at the world that came to life before me.

Rynmoor was a different city during the day. And then I realized.

Horses—even now, both of my worlds seemed to have so much in common.

I raced past the carriage as it slowed until it halted altogether, not bothering to see who stepped out of it and onto street. Not until he spoke.

"In a hurry, are you?" He quipped, and I looked back at him to see a man with dirty blond hair that fell just above his shoulders dressed in a trench coat as black as iron. His amber eyes widened when he saw me, truly caught sight of me for who he knew I was; but I didn't have any time. I opened my mouth to speak, but my legs carried me away before I could. The sun-drenched stone buildings blurred by as I ran, past the domes and arches and over the glass ferry that sailed beneath the Bridge of Water and Earth. The shadows of the trees swallowed me as the civilization of Rynmoor gave way to the serenity of the forest, and I called out my Old name without hesitation.

"Moonshadow!" I leapt into the golden wall of words and through the rift that opened up before me.

And I was instantly met with darkness.

"Connor?" I blinked, my eyes still adjusting to the inexplicable night.

How could it still be dark here if the sun had already risen in Rynmoor?

"Connor!" I yelled for him again when

the woods finally came into view.

There was no one else here.

"Connor!"

"Melissa," the sound of his voice brought the breath back into my lungs, "you're back. W—what happened?" He was holding his arms as he emerged from the trees to my left.

"What time is it?" He looked down at his wrist at my question, only to find that his father's watch was no longer there.

"Sorry." He sighed. "It's probably five o'clock, now."

"Five o'clock…" I whispered to myself, staring at the ground.

Rynmoor was three hours ahead.

"Where's Mr. Oakman?" I lifted my eyes to search the blackness for anything that might have betrayed him, but there was nothing.

"He left to take a couple blankets he brought out back to his boat. Why?" He gestured toward the lake before returning his attention to my face. And then to my dress. "What are you wearing?"

"It doesn't matter…" I breathed, grasping his hand. "We have to go." I pulled him towards the rift; but he hesitated, standing still.

"Whoa! Where are we going?" He exclaimed. "And what about the girls?"

"Rynmoor." I tried to explain, trying not to waste any time. "It's safe there. Heather and the others will be waiting." I paused when he suddenly loosened his grip and dropped his hand to his side. "Connor, we have to go!"

"Why would I want to go back?" I watched him shrug his shoulders and gaze up at the stars, and a sinister smile crept its way onto his face. "I like this place so much more." And then he stared at me, grinning as I looked at him in horror. He brought his hand back in a fist and struck my temple in a dizzying blow.

And everything went black.

"Melissa! Melissa!" My ears were ringing. "Melissa!" My eyes fluttered open as I lifted my head up from the ground, and I brushed off the dirt that had refused to leave my skin. I squinted my eyes at the figure running towards me, trying and failing to focus on its face. It grew bigger as it came closer; and it stumbled onto the forest floor beside me, placing its hands on my shoulders. "You've gotta stop making me chase you into dangerous situations."

Kana'ti.

"Sorry." I winced as he helped me up; but my knees buckled as I stood, and he kept me from falling.

"It was the Wendigo, wasn't it?" He didn't have to ask. I'm sure he already knew.

"Yeah." I held my hand to my forehead and grimaced, barely uttering the words.

"Connor — it's Connor."

"Are you sure?" I nodded my head as an answer. "Okay." The rustling of leaves in the distance sent him staring in the direction that it came from, and he took his bow from over his shoulder and nocked an arrow. A shape slowly revealed itself from the darkness of the trees that surrounded us; and I expected to see Connor's devilish smile, but it wasn't there. He was limping.

"Melissa..." His face was pale, as if he'd just seen something horrible. And the right leg of his jeans was soaked in blood. Kana'ti aimed the point of the arrow at his head, and Connor raised his hands in terror. "Caleb? How did you get here?"

"Stand back!" He commanded, and Connor reluctantly did as he asked.

"Melissa, it's me. I swear." He hurriedly stole a glance over his shoulder and brought his eyes back to me once again. He took a step forward, only to be met with a handful of light at the ready.

"How can I be sure?" I gazed at him, uncertain of what I should believe.

"Ask me something — anything." He stuttered, blinking his tired green eyes; and I stared into them in pursuit of something that I recognized.

"What did you say to me after you pulled me out of the water?" Kana'ti turned his head to look at me as I spoke. And a moment passed as I waited for his answer. Connor's eyes sparkled as he smiled a little, and I didn't even need to hear the words.

"I love you."

"Kana'ti, it's okay." I set my hand on his shoulder before racing to the edge of the clearing to wrap my arms around Connor's neck, and he grunted in pain. "I'm sorry." I let go, whispering. "I thought you were the Wendigo..." He wrinkled his forehead in confusion.

"What's a Wendigo?" He'd missed so much.

"It's an ice giant of the north woods," Kana'ti explained and joined us by the trees, "a shapeshifter that feeds on human flesh."

"Wait, what?" Connor asked, and I turned to face him.

"You didn't tell me that." I remarked, but he shook his head.

"It wasn't important at the time." I opened my mouth to respond, but Connor's voice kept me from speaking.

"If Mr. Oakman was this Wendigo the whole time, then why hasn't he already killed you?" It was a good question—one that I knew the answer to.

"He wants us all together..." I murmured, almost to myself; but the both of them heard me anyway.

"I offer you my congratulations." The three of us whirled in the direction of the voice to find what looked like Connor standing directly behind Kana'ti in the moonlight, and the grin he gave me sent a shiver down my spine. The Hunter pulled an arrow from the quiver on his back in an effort to strike him; but the Wendigo threw his hand across his chest, sending him hurdling into the pine tree and tumbling to the ground.

"Stay away from me!" I shouted and held my hand out to conjure up as much light as I could to keep him at bay, but he simply smiled and stepped towards me regardless of my warning.

"Or what?" He buried his hands in his pockets, eerily resembling the boy who had leaned against the lockers every morning before History class.

"I know who I am now!" I snapped at him and raised my voice, no longer trembling at the sight of him.

"Is that so?" He questioned me and narrowed his eyes, and it unsettled me how much I wanted to believe that it was Connor. But he was standing next to me—where he belonged.

"It is." I let the moonlight leave the palm of my hand and directed it towards him; and with a yelp of surprise, he collapsed when it hit his side. I stood there for a moment, stunned at what I had done; but Kana'ti stirred at the base of the pine tree, and I ran to him. "Are you okay?" I asked him as I helped him stand, and he nodded his head.

"It takes more than that." He reassured me.

"Good to know." I breathed.

Somehow, I kept forgetting what he was.

Connor hurried to join us and gestured to his doppelganger lying on the ground.

"It's not over." He warned us. I looked over to the Wendigo and immediately saw that he was right. It pulled itself up from the sylvan floor, clawing at the ground with hands that stretched and gnarled into bony fingers with nails like razors; and as it straightened its back to stand before me, I knew that I was seeing the monster that Kana'ti had described.

Like the skeleton of Crybaby Bridge, another stared back at me; but this one was so much more terrifying. It gazed through me with a pair of sunken yellow eyes, its shallow breaths pushing its leathery ash gray skin up from the ribs that encased its blackened lungs. The only hint of flesh was the stomach that protruded unnaturally from its gaunt figure, a sign that it would never be satisfied. It was riddled with abscesses and sores; and as it drew closer, the sickening stench of death and decay filled my nostrils. Wordless, it towered over me, rotting in the silence like a walking corpse; and I was horrified.

I lifted my hand again, nearly paralyzed by what I was seeing. And grinning, it seized my arm and threw me across the clearing, into the frigid dirt that I had found myself in more often than I would have liked. Before I could catch my breath, it wrapped its fingers around my neck and forced me against a bole of a tree; and it smiled with its tattered, bloody lips.

"I'm going to tear you in half," it savored the words as it spoke them in my ear; and only cold breath left its mouth and reached my cheek, "but not before your friends know the taste of your entrails." I whimpered as I pried at its fingers with my nails, ripping nothing but skin from its bones; but its inhuman strength was too much to overcome. It tightened its grip around my neck, and my lungs burned as I struggled to breathe. But suddenly, it lurched; and it turned its head as it released me, sending me dropping to my hands and knees. And I saw it as the creature faced its attacker.

An arrow.

"No more!" Kana'ti demanded, aiming another shaft at one of its eyes. "You've killed enough!" He shouted, and I crawled past the monster and into Connor's arms. In the darkness, I saw it smirk.

And I couldn't understand why.

"Not yet…" I could barely make out the words in its raspy voice before Connor called out my name in a panic, and I flailed my arm out for him desperately.

"Melissa!" Our fingers grasped for each other, but to no avail. And he was no longer beside me.

"Connor!" I screamed, hysterical. The Wendigo clutched his wrist and grinned with its graying teeth.

"One more…"

"Stop!" I shrieked, and everything was silent. Tears streamed down my cheeks as I watched Connor shake his head vehemently. "Stop." I whispered.

"Melissa, it — it's okay." Connor stuttered.

"No, it's not." I told him and stared into the Wendigo's yellow eyes. "You can have me." Kana'ti took a step forward, but I held him back. "Just let him go."

"Melissa, let me die—" He pleaded with me, but I wouldn't let him.

"No." I answered.

"Let me die!" He screamed at me, his voice cracking in his throat as he did. But I did everything I could to ignore him. The Wendigo beckoned for me as it nodded its head, loosening its hold on Connor as I moved towards it. But he gazed at me miserably, as if I were already dead. My heart beat loudly in my chest as I eliminated the space between us step by step, and the terror only magnified the sound.

This is it. This is how I'm going to die.

But I paused as I witnessed Connor move his lips, quietly but as clear as the night sky.

'I'm sorry.'

Before I could act, he pulled something out of his pocket; and a bright red flash erupted from whatever he had been holding. Tendrils of black smoke carried the smell of burning flesh to my nose, and I blinked away the tears that formed in my eyes.

"Connor?" I called his name, but he was staring at the object in his hand. "Connor?" He looked up at me in shock, not saying a word; and he staggered forward, my eyes widening in horror when his own didn't blink as he collapsed. "Connor!" I screamed, and the Wendigo let two small bones fall from its bloodstained claws and onto the ground. And it turned its back and bounded into the trees.

"Stay here!" Kana'ti told me, nocking another arrow before darting after the monster and leaving me in the silence.

Connor lay lifeless on his side, his back saturated in crimson around the gash where the Wendigo had torn part of his spine from his body.

I fell to my knees, gazing at Connor's face as his eyes stared blankly at the moss that climbed the roots of the pine tree; and I grasped his hand, squeezing it earnestly.

"You didn't have to…Why did you do it?" I sobbed and held him in my arms, knowing that it was my fault.

All that I had done to keep him safe—none of it mattered.

"Why did you do it?" I pounded his chest with my fist, as if my anger alone would bring him back. "Why did you do it?!" I caught sight of the flare gun lying beside him, and I picked it up and threw it as far from him as I could.

The air felt so much heavier, like it was crushing me underneath its weight; and as hard as I tried, I couldn't breathe. All sound had abandoned me, leaving only my own weeping for comfort; but it wasn't enough.

And I realized that drowning felt nothing like this.

Something bubbled inside me, burned through my veins. And it tore at my insides until there was nothing left but anger. And all I saw was white.

Slowly, I stood and walked through the clearing and into the shadows where the Wendigo had disappeared; and I found it several yards away and leaning against a tree for support, holding one of its claws over the wound that Connor had sacrificed himself to cause.

"Melissa, stay back!" Kana'ti stretched out his hand in warning and returned to his previous stance, raising his bow up from his side and shooting another arrow into the arm that covered its chest. But I continued, not missing a step, and finally stopped in between them. I lifted my right hand over my head and towards the sky, towards the moon; and as I brought it back to my face in the form of a fist, the silver light of the moon no longer fell through the canopy of the trees, leaving only darkness in its wake. Willfully, I uncurled my fingers to reveal the light of a thousand stars in the palm of my hand; and I set my eyes on the Wendigo with a grin. Kana'ti dropped the bow to shield his eyes from the light when it suddenly exploded, destroying every shadow in its path. I held up my hands as if I was rending the veil between worlds itself, but it was the Wendigo that was torn to pieces. Its yellow eyes filled with the radiance that I had unleashed upon it, and its skin tightened around its bones as it let out the most bloodcurdling shriek. One final chilling, animalistic wail erupted into the night as I erased it from existence; and when the light died down, there was nothing but ash and the smoldering tatters of its leathery skin drifting to the ground. The fire in my eyes was lost, and I looked to Kana'ti to see him staring at me in astonishment.

Or fear. I wasn't sure.

I left him standing there, the moon returning to the sky as I stepped backwards, breaking into a run to race back to Connor's body.

Healer's blood. It was the only thing I could hold onto.

I stumbled onto my knees and held my hands over his chest, letting everything I held inside me leave my fingertips. He convulsed with the sudden surge of energy, but nothing happened.

"Come on…" I murmured to him. I sent another blast of light through his system. "Come on." Again. "Come on!" Again. I gathered it all into my hands until it burned every cell in my fingers and released it, screaming from how much it hurt.

"Melissa!" Kana'ti took hold of my shoulders and shook me. "You can't bring back the dead! That's not your gift! Kaliveia, maybe, but not you!"

What good was it? What good could I do if I wasn't powerful enough to stop him from dying? The Morkoa were dead—all of them but me. And I was so alone.

He held me close as I sobbed, burying my face in his chest; and he kissed the top of my head and whispered.

"You are so much more than I could have ever imagined." He trembled, causing me to look up at his doleful eyes.

I hadn't seen him take the arrow from his quiver—or plunge it deep into where he had intended. But I had felt it.

"What have you done?" I caught him as he swayed forward, growing limp in my arms; and I gazed down at the fatal wound that he had inflicted on himself.

"You need him more." A tear streamed down his face as I held him; and he flashed me a clever grin as he caressed my cheek. A soft breeze whipped up his dark brown hair; and he vanished into a wave of golden sparks, carried away into the darkness with the wind. I sat there—in the quietness, staring at the place where he had been.

Two hundred years.

I jumped when Connor's body suddenly gasped for air behind me, wheezing and coughing in a panic. And I turned to look at him as the last of hundreds of embers tumbled from his skin and out of existence, not sure if it was real.

But it was.

"Connor!" I breathed as I scrambled to his side, and I clutched his hand in an effort to calm him. "It's okay." I reassured him. "I'm here." I couldn't keep myself from smiling. My tears fell from my eyes and found their place on his cheeks, streaking his muddy face as they rolled away and onto the ground.

"Melissa!" The both of us lifted our heads at the sound of Heather's voice, and we watched as she and the others came bursting out of the rippling veil. Her pale green eyes widened when she caught sight of us; and she darted to where Connor lay, kneeling beside him. "What happened?" She asked me, horrified, and turned her head in search of my Kindred. "Where's Kana'ti?"

"He," I swallowed, "he's gone. Something attacked us and—" I stopped when Connor shakily squeezed my hand. Whimpering, he lifted his other hand up from the ground and pointed; and instantly, I knew what it was.

I whirled to face the cloaked figure of the Ravenmocker hovering over us, floating silently in the blackness of the night.

"I can see it, too." Heather said, in a disbelief of what her life had come to be. From what I could make out of its warped visage, it seemed to open its mouth in a wrathful scream; and I held up my hand as it rushed towards us.

But nothing happened.

I looked up when it screeched in frustration, charging at me again and again with no success. Something I couldn't see stopped it from coming any farther—like a shield—an invisible barrier. It let out a shrill cry as it incinerated from the inside, and I covered my eyes as it was engulfed in flames. I lowered my hand when it was finally gone, only to see a girl dressed in pink standing before me. A tall young man crowned with a head of curly dark brown hair emerged from the trees to join her.

He looked familiar; but so much had

happened, I couldn't remember where I had seen him.

She hurried through the remaining wisps of smoke and drifting ashes to bend down to my level.

"Are you all right?" She gingerly placed her hand on my arm, her voice burdened with worry. I nodded my head before looking at Connor from over my shoulder, and she glanced at him before calling the young man's name. "Pierre, we have a problem." He frowned; and when he spoke as he joined us, I knew.

"Is it serious?" He paused the moment he saw the gash in Connor's back. "Oh."

"We'll have to leave sooner than I thought." Dorothy sighed, and Heather's head perked up at her words.

"Leave?" She asked what all of us were wondering.

"There's a place where people like us go to be safe." She explained. "We can help him there."

"People like us?" I peered at her, more confused than I'd ever been.

I wasn't sure if there was anyone I could trust anymore.

"You said you were from Massachusetts."

"I didn't lie." She responded, solemn. "I was born in Salem in 1688." I opened my mouth to speak—to ask her another question; but she wouldn't let me. "There's no time. I'll explain when we get there." She gazed up at the eleven girls standing around us as they shivered in the darkness. "There's room for all of you." She assured them, but Heather took my hand and smiled sadly.

"I think I've had enough adventure." She started, squeezing my fingers as she held back the tears that refused to stay in her eyes. "Go. We'll stay."

"Are you sure?" Everything in me wanted to fall apart. I had done so much to get her back; and now, we'd fallen back to the beginning.

"Yeah." She nodded, but her voice said something else completely. "This town's got a few more mysteries for me." She chuckled a little, if only to keep herself from crying. "Go." She insisted and pulled me into a hug that never wanted to end. But we let go, and I felt a piece of me leave with her. Dorothy fished her hand into the pocket of her coat and retrieved a silver necklace that sparkled in the moonlight.

The pendant was shaped like a flattened explorer's globe on a diagonal axis, and I realized that she was wearing its twin around her neck.

"Take this." She set it carefully in Heather's hand. "And when you need us, we will come." She promised her, something that I'm sure she didn't take lightly.

"Thank you." Heather closed her fingers around it.

"There's a boat at the edge of the woods." Pierre added, and she grinned at me one last time.

"I guess this is goodbye." She sighed.

"For now." I answered, and she nodded her head.

"For now."

"Engage." Dorothy spoke, touching her necklace; and I waved goodbye as Heather and Charlotte and all of the others faded from my sight.

Epilogue

$\mathcal{E}$verything was white — like we were trapped in a snowstorm, or the middle of a star.

Stars. That's what they looked like.

The massive room took shape around us — every line, every tile on the floor. And in the center, a silver statue of the Earth spun slowly, covered in a million bright lights. There were people, sitting at what I could only guess were radar screens. Five — each of them more different than the next. Several pairs of legs rushed past me, and I realized that I was still sitting on the ground — next to Connor.

"I'll get a wheelchair." Pierre told us and darted toward the eastern wall, disappearing behind its only door.

"You were alive during the witch trials." I thought aloud, and Dorothy nodded.

"I was. My mother, Sarah Good, died

ensuring my safety." She replied. "They were right to be afraid — but *I* was the one they should have been afraid of." Pierre's quick steps echoed in my ears when he returned with the wheelchair, and the both of us helped Connor up from the floor and into his seat.

"Follow me." He said and took hold of the handles to push him in the direction that he had gone before. Dorothy turned the knob and pulled the door open, revealing a room filled with beds that lined opposite walls and white curtains that fell between them. A man with dark hair that fell just above his shoulders sauntered towards us and urgently gestured for us to join him.

"Come quickly." There was an accent in his voice — English — or maybe something else entirely. The four of us followed him to an empty mattress, where two other people were waiting; and two of the strangers carried Connor from the wheelchair to the white sheets of the hospital bed.

"Thank you." I breathed, turning to face a man in his mid-twenties and a girl no older than sixteen with golden brown hair.

"O' course." He responded with a heavy New Jersey accent, and I grinned when I recognized the city boy in him. "James Duncan." He introduced himself. "And this here's Agnus." He gestured to her as she handed the doctor a roll of bandages.

"Nice to meet you." I reached out to shake her hand; but she struggled to find it, her amber eyes searching but failing. The blood rose to my face, and I grasped her hand when I realized that she was blind. "I'm sorry. I didn't…"

"It's all right." She smiled. "James forgets all the time."

"Where are ya from?" James inquired, and I hesitated.

It was weird—meeting all of these people—answering their questions.

"Oklahoma," I started, correcting myself, "Xaijena. It's complicated." He grinned.

"Ain't it always?" He walked around me to reach the other side of the bed. "Jersey, 1924. Robert's been all over. Ain't that right, Doctor?"

"Wait…" Agnus lifted her head up from her work. "Did you say 'Xaijena'?"

"I did." I responded; and for the first time, I truly saw her eyes—the same eyes that I had seen on that road in Rynmoor—in the man dressed in black.

"Melissa Moonwater?" A hush fell over the room at the sound of a woman's voice, and I turned to face the source of it.

There was something about her—something I couldn't explain; but the mystery only magnified how enchanting she was. She was dressed in blue, green, and gold—like a princess of Persia; and two gold hoop earrings hid within her dark brown wavy hair. She wasn't the eldest. I could tell. But there was something old in her eyes, as if she held a wisdom no one else could understand.

"Yes?" It was frightening — the moment she looked at me. But she grinned invitingly and beckoned for me to join her.

"My name is Andromeda." She paused, stealing a glimpse at the door. "Would you come with me?" I faltered at her words. "He's in safe hands. I promise." I gazed at her, uncertain; but nothing in her voice hinted of anything other than the truth.

"O — okay." I stuttered, and I followed her as she left the infirmary to walk across the room that I had first come to. There, in the opposite wall, stood a door in the very middle and two others where the north and south walls met; and I wondered where each of them led to. We stopped at the one in the center, and she smiled at me before pushing it open. I stepped into a spacious corridor, where the echoes of my footsteps reverberated off the walls and grasped at my hair.

It was silent, in a reverent kind of way — as if I had set foot in a crypt of kings.

"Pierre, Dorothy, Marco, and I built these walls." She ran her fingers along the wooden panels as she walked past me and towards the center of the room. My eyes drifted to a head of blond hair idling by the wall a few yards away from me, and I couldn't keep from staring. There was something in his hand.

A handful of feathers? No. It was a duster.

He glanced at me from over his shoulder, and then at the woman who had led me here.

"Andromeda..." He beamed. "Is it true?"

"For another time, Luke." She grinned. "Would you grant us the room, if you please?"

"Of course." He nodded and turned to me with a salute. "Auf Wiedersehen." In a flash, he was gone, the outline of his body blurring past me and sending my hair flying around my face. I gazed at the open doorway in awe, barely able to speak.

"Whoa..."

"Most of us are Mythborn: children of beings that the world has long forgotten." I whirled to face her as she continued. "Others — like Luke — they were born powerless...but chosen. But *you*," she paused as she looked at me, as if she were seeing something she hadn't seen in a long time, "you're different."

"How?" I wanted to know — so desperately.

How far down did this well reach?

She stole a step forward.

"You're what we call a Radiant: a child of the stars. A being of immeasurable power, unspeakable influence. Someone who can shift worlds — tear the universe apart. I know Dorothy gave you a choice, but I want to be sure that you know what I am asking of you." She said, and I took in a deep breath as she drew closer. "I'd like to invite you to join us. There are more people out there like us—like you. But there are forces that wish to see them destroyed, and I will not allow that. This place was meant to be a haven that people could come to, but I've found recently that it's not that simple."

"Like me..." I marveled to myself, struggling to understand what that meant.

For me. For Connor. For this place that I'd just begun to experience.

"Will you help us?" She asked, and my response nearly overlapped her question.

"Yes." I answered her.

I didn't have to think about it. This was what I wanted.

"Well, then..." She smiled. "Welcome to Star Corps."

Acknowledgements

There are quite a few that I would like to thank for walking with me on this journey, but I would like to start with my first librarian, Mr. Alex Vargas. You spun magic with your words and captivated my mind with the power of your storytelling, and in doing so, inspired a heart for telling my own stories. Thank you for instilling that in me.

To my English teachers who recognized my talent for writing and devoted their time to help sharpen my skills, but especially to Mrs. Purvis and Ms. Perry — thank you for pulling me aside to share your confidence in my abilities. You gave me the reassurance that I needed when I doubted myself. A very special thank you to my beta reader, Michael Mahnke. You gave me the last bit of confidence I needed to know that this was always what I was meant to be.

Kodey Bell, a.k.a. Imaginesto, thank you for providing me with a beautiful cover for my book. You captured the spirit of my story perfectly with your work, and I am so very thankful for your contribution. To my professional photographer, Darlene Platt of Platt Photography, thank you for taking the picture now featured on my author page. Thank you, Dillon Barker, for helping me create said author page and advising me in all social media and advertising aspects.

My dear friends, Melissa De Jesus and Heather Current, I am so grateful for you both and your willingness to lend your names to this story. This book is a testament to my love for you. My writing buddies: fellow author Steven Shinder, budding screenwriter Melissa Sifuentes, and beloved and since past Yasmen Vidales— growing alongside you has been an honor I will hold close to my heart.

To Alexa, my sister, thank you for sticking with me through long nights staring at my laptop and my endless questions regarding my creative choices—even though our brains work best at opposite times of the day. And for absorbing me into your very own Dead Poets Society. The ideas for Moonshadow were born in that high school classroom. And Mom, thank you for supporting me in everything that I do and fostering a love for reading very early on in my childhood. For every book you read with me before bed, every short story you looked over when I was just beginning to put my imagination to paper, and every silent hour we sat together in the living room on Saturday afternoons — enjoying the books we just procured from the Borders around the corner from dance class.

About the Author

Krystina Coles was born in 1995 in San Diego, California. Though she graduated in 2014 as a chef in the art of baking and pastry, writing and telling stories was always her greatest passion. When she is not writing poetry or sewing elaborate costumes, she can be found baking desserts for her loved ones. She continues to live in her hometown of San Diego with her family and her dog, Chipper, and works with elementary through high school age children.

Made in the USA
San Bernardino, CA
01 February 2020

63875844R00197